MARY WATSON

M o s s

95627 - Feb. 2007

KWELA BOOKS

This publication was supported by the
National Arts Council of South Africa

NATIONAL **ARTS** COUNCIL
OF SOUTH AFRICA

Cover design by Alexander Kononov
Typography by Nazli Jacobs
Set in Bembo
Printed and bound by Paarl Print,
Oosterland Street, Paarl, South Africa

First edition, first printing 2004

ISBN 0-7957-0181-0

http://www.kwela.com

3 5944 00095 6274

For the oracle, a coven of sisters, my mother & k.

Contents

J u n g f r a u

It was the Virgin Jessica who taught me about wickedness. I once asked her why she was called the Virgin Jessica. She looked at me with strange eyes and said that it was because she was a special person, like the Blessed Mary.

"A virgin is someone who can do God's work. And if you're very, very clean and pure you can be one of the one hundred and forty-four virgins who will be carried in God's bosom at the end of the world. And if you're not —"

She leaned towards me, her yellow teeth before my eye. I thought she might suck it out, she was so close. She whispered, "If you're not, then God will toss you to the devil who will roast you with his horn. Like toasted marshmallows. You don't want the devil's evil horn to make a hole in your pretty skin, now do you?"

She kissed my nose — my little rabbit's nose, she called it — and walked away, her long white summer dress falling just above her high, high red heels. Her smell, cigarette smoke and last night's perfume, lingered around my eyeball. I wanted to be like the Virgin Jessica. I wanted a name like hers.

We called her Jez for short.

My mother, Annette, was the Virgin Jessica's adopted sister. She was older and tireder. The Virgin had no children while my mother had forty-three. She was a schoolteacher in one of those schools where the children wore threadbare jerseys and had hard green snot crystallised around their noses and above their crusty lips — lips that could say *poes* without tasting any bitterness. Or that secret relish of forbidden language.

Sometimes my mother would have them — her other children, her little smelly children — over at our house. They would drape them-

9

selves around our furniture like dirty ornamental cherubs and drink hot pea soup. The steam melted the snot, which then ran down into the soup. It did not matter to them because they ate their boogers anyway.

I hated my mother's other children. I glared at them to let them know, but they stared back without much expression. Their faces had nothing to say – I could read nothing there. Jessica found them amusing.

"Sweet little things," she mumbled, and laughed into her coffee. Her shoulders shook epileptically.

After the Virgin told me how important it was to be clean, I tolerated them in the haze of my superiority. I was clean – I bathed every night – and they were filthy, so obviously God wouldn't want to touch them.

The Virgin spent hours in the bathroom every evening. Naked she walked to her bedroom, so lovely and proud she seemed tall; I followed faithfully, to observe a ritual more awesome than church. With creams and powders she made herself even cleaner for God. How he must love her, I thought. She spread his love upon her as she rubbed her skin until it glowed and her smell spread through the house, covering us all with the strength of her devotion. Then she went out, just after my father came home, and stayed out until late.

The Virgin Jessica had a cloud of charm twenty centimetres around her body. Strangers hated her because they thought that anyone that beautiful could only be mean. But it wasn't her pretty black eyes or her mouth that made her beautiful. She was beautiful because she was wrapped in a cloud of charm. And when you breathed in the air from the cloud, you breathed in the charm and it went down your veins and into your heart and made you love her. If you came close enough, she would smile her skew smile, pretending to love you with her slitted eyes, and the charm would ooze out like fog from a sewer and grab you and sink into your heart and lungs. Even I who had known her all my life would feel the charm with a funny ache. She had a way of leaning forward when she spoke, claiming the space around her with her smell, her charm. And my father, who didn't speak or laugh, he too would be conquered.

"What's the old man up to tonight?" she would say, leaning towards him with a wink, her eyes laughing; and he would fold his newspaper and look pleased, even grunt contentedly.

I tried saying those same words, leaning forward the way Jez did, and he looked at me coldly. So cold that my wink froze halfway and my laugh caught in my throat. Embarrassed, I transformed the laugh into a cough and rubbed my eyes like a tired child. I think it was then that I realised that his love for me was bound to me as his little girl. And my love for him bound me to my little girl's world.

I took pains to keep my girl's world intact after that. When boys teased me at school, I felt the walls of my father's favour tremble. One of them phoned and sang a dirty song into my hot ear. My head burnt for days after that. I felt the fires of hell from that phone call. I feared that the fires would start inside me, catching my hair and eating the strands like candlewick, melting my skin like wax, dripping and staining mommy's carpets (she would be very cross). The fire would eat the horrid children in the schoolroom, then crawl towards my mother, burn her slowly and then finish with her chalk-stained fingers. Her glasses would shrivel up and her mouth crease with silent screams. Unsatisfied, the fire would move towards my father, crackling his newspaper; the smoke would cloud his glasses. Beneath them, his eyes would have that same cold look – but not cold enough to douse the flames. The fire would then stagger towards the Virgin. Leering, it would grab her ankles and eat her white frock, turning it to soot. She would cry out and her head would toss, her hair unravel and she would scream from the force of the flames. The Virgin Jessica's screams in my head made me put a knife on the windowsill of her bedroom so that she could undo the burglar bars and escape.

The image of flames and screams resounded in my head for several days. They surged whenever the other girls in their shortened school dresses lit cigarettes in the toilets. They could not see how the flames would get bigger. I checked all the stubs carelessly tossed into the sink and bin to make sure that the fire did not escape. The slight thrill I had once received from the boys teasing me in the safety of the schoolyard, away from my father's fearsome eyes, faded. I spent my intervals at the far end of the yard, eating sandwiches and talking to the dogs through the wire fence. I had to coax them across the road with my milk and the ham from my bread. I was found one day, squatting on my haunches and telling Nina and Hildegarde about a garden of moss. I felt a shadow; it made me shiver, and I looked up to see if God was angry. Instead I saw Ms Collins above me, her eyes made huge by her glasses. I was scared that she'd be cross. I wanted to pee; some dripped down my leg, so I crouched and shut my eyes tightly, praying fervently that I would not pee. She reached out for my hand and asked me to make some charts for her in exchange for some biscuits and cooldrink. From then on I spent my breaks helping Ms Collins in her art room and she would give me yoghurt and fruit and sometimes chocolate. I never ate these. Instead I put them on the steps of the white Kirk on the way home. Ms Collins tried to ask me questions, but I was shy and would only whisper, "I don't know." She would speak relentlessly. She told me about her baby daughter who ate grass.

I preferred just to look at her. I liked looking at her big ugly eyes and her pretty hair. But I think she got tired of me: maybe my silence wore her down, maybe the sound of her own voice scared her, for it must have been like talking to herself. She probably thought she was going mad, talking and talking to still brown eyes. But the day I went into her art room and found a boy from my class helping her with the charts, I remembered the fires of hell and ran away. Maybe she wanted me to burn; maybe she wasn't a virgin either.

It must have been the sound of midnight that woke me. The house without my mother felt unguarded. It seemed her presence warded off a fury of demons. I sat upright in my clean girl's bed, trying to feel the pulse of the night. I slipped my feet over the side of the bed and listened. The darkness is covered by a haze that makes the still corners move.

I knew that my mother had not returned. The wild child with snot streaming from his nose and eyes, he had her still. I sat at the lounge window, watching the sea, hating the wild child. He had come after supper, his little body panting like a steam engine. He ran up the hill in the rain, he had run all the way from the settlement. He sobbed, buried his head in my mother's trousers.

"Please, please, *asseblief,* please," his broken voice scratched.

Wishing so very hard that he hadn't come, I watched the boy cry until my mother barked, "Evelyn, get out of here."

I prayed that the wild child would leave: go back to your plague, I screamed silently. It was too late. He had brought his plague with him. It wandered about our house and muffled my warnings. So she did not hear me, and let the child take her away.

Her trousers soiled with tears and mucus, she rushed into her bedroom, where I was watching one of those endless sitcoms about silly teenagers. She grabbed her car keys.

"Don't wait up for me."

I would not have waited for her. Even now, in the dark hour, I was not waiting for her.

I must have stayed at the window for at least an hour. I saw the sea roar-smash-roar against the rocks. I saw the stillness of the midnight road, the white line running on towards the mountain. The road was empty; but then I saw two people walking up the hill. They walked slowly and closely in their midnight world. The walk was a stagger. They fell pleasantly against each other. I saw them walk towards the house and only then did I see who they were.

When Jessica and my father entered the house, quietly and with the guilty grace of burglars, they were glowing from the wind and walking and waves and the wildness of the night's beauty. The haze inherent in the darkness was centred around them. I looked on with envy, for I too wished to walk the empty night with them.

Jessica let out a startled sound when she saw me curled up on the window-sill.

"Look at you," she fussed, "hanging around dark windows like a sad little ghost."

Her face was close to mine and her breathing deep.

"Have you been watching for your mother? Has she come home yet?"

I shook my head. I had not been waiting for my mother.

She held my hands in her cold, cold fingers. "Your hands are freezing," she said.

"You need some Milo. How long have you been sitting here? Long? Your father and I went to see if your mother was coming home. I wish she'd phone, but then they probably don't have one. I really don't understand why Annette involves herself in other people's business. But I suppose you should count your blessings. When we were small, your mother and me, all we had to play with was scrap metal."

Jessica chattered on, repeating the stories I had heard so many times.

My mother came home while I was clutching my Milo. I was playing the mournful ghost, the sick patient, and all the while glowing in the attention of both my father and Jessica. Jessica was chattering brightly, so bright that she made the darkness her own while I huddled in its shadows. My father was silent, his eyes as dark as mine. Jessica's words tripped out of her mouth and drew circles around us.

Then Annette stepped into our enchanted circle. She asked for tea. As Jessica made the tea her words stumbled then stopped. My father went to bed, taking my hand as he left the kitchen. I did not want to go to bed. I wanted to be in the kitchen with just my father and Jessica and me.

I stood on a rock in the garden and stared down at the people watching my sea. They were dotted across the small beach, the wind twisting their hair around their necks and forcing them closer into their jackets. They lifted their fingers to point, just like in a seaside painting. Their mouths were wide with laughter and their eyes bright, yet all the while I knew that they were posing, as if for an invisible artist. Their minds could sometimes glimpse his black beret, his paint-splattered smock in this idyllic scene.

I went down to the sea. There were too many whale watchers trampling the sand, my desecrated temple, with their flat feet and stubby toes. I glared at the fat children who clung to their parents, hanging on to their arms and legs.

"Beast with two backs," I muttered.

They smelt suburban. Their odour of white bread and Marmite drifted unpleasantly into the sea air. They huddled into their windbreakers and yawned at the ocean.

"It's just a dark blob," they whined, their winter-paled faces cracking beneath the noon sun. They shivered from the wind nuzzling their necks.

I sat near the water's edge and buried my pretty toes in the sand. The crowd, the people who came to see the whales, were noisy and their noise ate into my ears as they crunched their chips and the packets crackled in the wind.

"Go home," I hissed to a solitary toddler who wandered near me.

I turned to see a woman scoop him up and pretend to eat his angel curls. My coward's face smiled at her.

I stayed there for a while, watching the people watch the whales. Then I noticed some of my mother's children playing in the water on the other side of the beach. They shrieked and laughed; some played in their dirty clothes, others in varying stages of nakedness. They sang a ditty with filthy words while roughly shoving and splashing each other with the cold water. They knocked down their friends and made them eat sand. The suburban children's parents shook their heads, pulled their young ones and walked away, still shaking their heads, as though the shaking would dispel the image from their minds. They soon forgot all about those children who haunted the corners of my world, my mother's chosen children.

15

She came to call me for lunch. She did not see her young ones, who had moved towards the tidal pool, and I did not tell her about them.

I sneaked my mother off the beach, chattering too brightly. We walked towards the hill. Someone came running behind us, but we carried on walking, for my mother didn't seem to hear the footsteps – maybe I was too bright. I walked faster and we crossed Main Road. When we reached the other side, I felt a light strong-hard knock like a spirit just made solid. I turned to see the wild child hugging my mother, her arms wrapped around him. He gave her a flower and ran back. When the wild child crossed the road, he was hit by whale people in a blue car. The driver got out, my mother ran to her child. The driver, annoyed and red, complained that he hadn't seen anyone, there was nobody there.

"Just a shadow flitted across my eyes," his wife wailed. "Just a dark shadow."

The driver said that he would fetch help. He and his wife drove off in their blue car – the dent was slight – and didn't come back. Perhaps to him there really was nobody there: the dent was so very slight, and those children are so thin, after all.

My mother lifted the wild child in her arms. She waited and while she waited, her mouth got tighter and tighter and she wept. When one hundred blue cars had passed by, she slowly got up from the pavement. With the wild child in her arms, she walked up the hill. She did not speak to me, her mouth was tight and her hair unbound from its ponytail.

At our house Jessica and my father hovered awkwardly around her, their legs and arms looking wrong on their bodies, as if they had taken them off and put them back the wrong way. They moved slowly and clumsily, like they had wound down. My mother lay her child on my clean girl's bed and stayed by his side.

"Stephen, get the doctor quickly," she barked at my father.

I ate my Sunday roast. I paid little attention to the doctor's arrival or the child's crying or my mother's pacing. Her tight face had shut me out. I sat in the lounge and watched the sea, picking at the meat. When the violet hour came, the beach was empty and my room smelt of the wild child and the barest hint of my mother's love. But they were both gone.

I stayed in the lounge with my father and the Virgin, who brought us tea. We played cards and laughed the soft, covered laughs of forbidden frivolity. We munched biscuits and watched the Virgin's teasing eyes as she tried to cheat, as she toasted marshmallows over a candle flame, as she spoke, smiled, sighed. The wild child and my mother were forgotten. I did not think of the bruised bundle on my bed.

Then the quiet beneath our laughter became too insistent. It was guilt that sent me in search of her. It was the guilt of the betrayer for the betrayed, because guilt is more binding than passion.

There was not a trace of my mother and the wild child in my bedroom. There was no mark of my mother's care or her chosen child's blood staining the sheets. There were no cup rings on my dressing table, no dent on the pillow. I looked for my mother in my bedroom. I hunted in every corner but could not find the slightest whisper of her smell.

I could find nothing of her in the lounge – that was my father's room. Their bedroom was green and clinical and did not contain either of them. The kitchen was heavy with the Virgin's presence, which smelt of rose water with a burny undertone. I sat down on the floor, perplexed.

Agitated, I realised that I could not remember if her smell had been in the house the day before. Or the previous week. I went to the garage, which she used as a schoolroom. As I opened the door, a fury of smells came screaming towards me. There were the wild children's smells of pain and fear and anger. And she was there, entangled in this foul mix. Nothing of her remained in the house because it was all concentrated here. Delicately it cushioned and enveloped the rawness of the children as it wove itself into them. The force of this beauty, this tenderness made me want to weep with jealousy. Such sadness, such terror. I left the dim garage knowing that my mother had been gone for a long time. I had not noticed because I had been coveting the Virgin. I went back to the house.

Jessica tilted her head slightly and focused her skew eyes on me. I had not seen her standing in the doorway, slim and graceful (she was so beautiful), watching me.

"What are you sniffing around for? Does something smell bad?" She seemed anxious.

"Not in here," I replied. "I was just smelling. Smelling to see where my mother has gone."

"You funny, funny child," she said, wrapping her precious arms around me. I pretended to squirm. "What else can that incredible snout of yours sniff out? Can you smell where your father is?"

I was surprised, because she didn't understand me at all. I looked at her and saw an odd dullness in her pretty face.

"It doesn't happen with my nose," I tried to explain. "It happens inside somewhere, same as when Daddy and I go to the moss garden. I don't see it with my eyes."

She regarded me with a slight frown shadowing her eyes and making her face sulky.

"What moss garden?"

"Secrets."

I smiled sweetly at her and she lost her frown and said, "Don't you trouble your pretty little head about your inner eyes and ears, you are much too young for such worries."

She coaxed me into helping her make sandwiches, which was easy because I loved doing anything with her. But she still did not know what I meant.

I sought out my mother after that. I lavished attention upon her, for I felt that I had betrayed her. I betrayed her with my unholy, selfish love for the Virgin. I placated her with tokens of love, with tea and wild flowers picked along the road to the beach. I feared that the

18

Blessed Mary would not be pleased that in my heart of hearts I had turned my love from my flesh mother to another. My guilt was augmented by my jealousy of her chosen children, and because I denied her my love yet begrudged her theirs. As my guilt grew so her nocturnal visits to the township increased.

"There's so much fear out there, you couldn't imagine it, Evie. You're a lucky, lucky girl. I remember being so poor that my hunger nearly drove me insane. We were like wild flowers growing on the side of the road."

I resented my mother's childhood poverty. I resented her hunger and I resented being made to feel guilty about not being hungry.

"You could so easily have been one of those children, look at Auntie Carmelita, the way her children run around, that's the inmates ruling the asylum. So you just be grateful that you're not like them. You think about that if it makes you sad when I go out at night."

It did not make me sad when she went out at night. I was jealous but not sad, because her absence set my nights free. I would stare at the midnight sea; I would walk the moss garden with my father.

I sought her greedily with endless cups of tea and awkwardly asked her how her day had been – did she not think the weather was fine for this time of year? – smoothed her hair, kissed her cheek with my Judas lips and fussed about her as much as Jessica did.

And she would be propped in her chair, my mother, my failed heroine, and I would talk and talk and she would say, "Not now, Evie, I'm tired, tired," and my guilt would grow and I would leave unhappy yet relieved. Her eyes would hold mine and she would say, "Thanks Evie," and the guilt grew and grew because there was trust and affection in her eyes, doggy brown eyes that I did not want to love.

Those eyes changed one day and she became cross. Her breath was thin and tinny, like she did not want to take air in, let air out. The tedium of breathing seemed to offend her, so she resisted it. That was when she started smoking cigarettes. She took some of Jessica's cigarettes, shrugged like Jessica and laughed.

"Makes breathing interesting," she tittered. "Besides, we're all going to die anyway," she cackled, looking at the danger signs on the box. She laughed and laughed but it was a cross laugh.

It crept out of the silences, was born between a glance held, then turned away. This guilt would not be contained. It was in the air as plain as the tingling cold of sunny winter days. It kept me awake those cold August nights. So cold that my fingers would ache as I lay awake, feeling the ice in the walls, the breathing of the house, the numbness of my mother's nocturnal absences. I sighed and turned the other cheek, hoping to find sleep with my back to the wall, then my face, then my back again.

There is no rest for the wicked.

"Be a good girl," my father had said as he kissed me that night. "Be a good girl for your old father."

He kissed me again and pulled the covers up to my chin. When he got up from the bed, the mattress rose as the weight lifted. I felt safe then, as the rain and wind struck down on the roof.

It was still raining as I lay staring at the ceiling in the small hours of the morning.

There is no rest for the wicked.

Sighing an old woman's sigh, I kicked my tired sore legs to the right, the side where I always raised myself from the bed. I wandered to the kitchen seeking leftovers from the Virgin's dinner, because I was famished. Trying to be the good child exhausted me and then left me sleepless. I could hear my father snoring. He sounded like a wailing wolf. I was surprised that he slept. When I wandered around the rooms at night, I felt the alertness of a house that did not slumber nor sleep.

I found the Virgin in her kitchen. She was eating. She stuck her fork into the mince and rammed it into her mouth. Again and again she stuffed forkfuls into her mouth, sometimes pausing to mix the mince with spaghetti, her delicate fingers swiftly swirling it around the fork. The apple-pie dish lay empty before her.

When she looked up and saw me, spaghetti was hanging down the side of her mouth, from those sweet red lips. She let go of the fork. She seemed embarrassed, but she had no need to be because I knew that she had been fasting. The virgin often fasted to deny herself the pleasures of the flesh. I admired her for that because I could not fast no matter how hard I tried. But looking at her with spaghetti on her chin and mince on her white nightgown, I felt ill. Surely she would make herself sick, eating like that. She looked up and saw me, and it frightened me because she looked old. The guilt had etched itself there too. I was frightened because I thought that the Virgin was pure. I chased those naughty thoughts from my mind. I chased them until my beloved virgin seemed young again. Then unbidden, the words came to my mouth.

"There's no rest for the wicked," I said.

My words hurt her; she placed her head in her hands. The guilt was what made me do it, the guilt, it made words come to my mouth. My secret joy at releasing suppressed words sank into my flesh and I felt my skin tauten. My hands were wet so I wiped my mouth, but it would not be clean. When she left the room, my mind screamed for her mercy, for forgiveness. She did not hear me; she took none of that with her. I sat in her chair and waited and waited.

I longed for my mother then. I longed to press my burning face, my wet nose into her trousers and sob. I wanted her to leave her bed at night and come to me and to choose me as her child and I would choose her as my mother and the guilt would go away and we would be happy. I went to where I knew I would find some of her.

The schoolroom door creaked slightly and my white slippers upon the cold cement floor made a featherlight crunch. I stood in the dark waiting to feel her and the children, waiting for sounds that were long gone. I crossed my arms around myself and waited. And then they came to me – the sighs, the hushed tinkles of laughter, the moans and the whimpers. The room was drenched in sorrow. I listened excitedly as the ghosts of yesterday came to me. The sounds grew less and less faint. They were calling to me. The shadows started taking shape and I saw that everything had fallen into a woven mass, a moving tapestry in the corner of the schoolroom. I saw my mother as a she-wolf, her hair tangled and glowing, licking her young ones, her tongue moving over furry flesh. I wanted to join her pack and have her lick my sins away. I moved towards them, then stopped, for the shadows changed again. My mother now had Jessica's face, an unfamiliar Jessica face with enormous slanted glowing eyes, feral biting teeth that dipped to the whimpering flesh beneath her. My mother was gone.

"Mommy?" I whispered. "Mommy?" It was shrill and anxious. I did not know what magic I had conjured.

"Mommy?"

Everything stopped moving. The tapestry froze and then unravelled.

And then I saw them. I had not imagined the moving tapestry in the corner of the schoolroom, nor had I imagined Jessica licking the furry flesh. As my eyes accustomed themselves to the dim light, I saw that it was my father with Jessica. They were clumsily covering their bodies, hiding themselves, and I thought that was silly – I had seen it all before. But I had not known that he shared the moss garden with her. I left the garage. I heard them calling after me and I walked away.

Jessica Without Detail

(told to Sean the furniture-repossession man and artist by the
Virgin Jessica)

Mr Warlock's girls breathed in tin and rust from the scrap metal in their backyard. The scrap fed them and clothed them. Their breath was thin and tinny, but they remembered a time when there hadn't been enough food – they weren't allowed to forget. So they inhaled corrosive dust every time they opened their windows and they did not complain. There were six of them, the Warlock girls, and they were lovely. At times they were seen with straight backs and keen eyes at Our Lady of Sorrows. Their ardour strained through each earnest hymn, but the girls sang, even spoke with the breathless wheeze of rusted scrap. Other times they were seen squashed into the primrose-yellow Mercedes Benz with their flowered church hats hiding their faces. As the bulky yellow car bore the girls away, the neighbourhood children – orange from the unpaved roads – danced aside to avoid the flying gravel. The girls sat quietly in the back seat as they sailed through Grassy Park.

There may have been a few tenacious weeds pushing through the cracks in the pavement, some errant Port Jackson trees in the sandy fields, but Grassy Park seemed an unkind name. The forlorn gardens bore mostly daisy bushes which (with occasional archways) had lent roundness to the square imagination of some apartheid architect. They drove past the no-good boys who always leaned against the wall of the Elite Supermarket and called out to the girls passing by. Sheila told her girls that these boys were up to no good, hanging around like that. All they wanted to do was get young girls pregnant and then not marry them. The boys whistled and bowed mockingly. The sisters averted their eyes. What troubled them about the no-good boys was not so much their no-good desires but that they just stood against that wall: didn't they get bored doing nothing?

Then they drove past the council flats – there were rows and rows of them in dreary grey and piled too closely. Offended by such colourless regularity, the girls never failed to close their windows. Even the graffiti was uninspired. Instead of bold swirls of rebellion, the walls carried only sickly twists of black spray-paint.

"Vain scribblings," Sheila muttered crossly from the front seat. "Up to no good."

Their own house, just on the other side, was curiously stacked. It had grown up in the last seven years to be a strange mix of metal and brick. The backyard was a forest of metal trees in cement earth. Here iron clashed against iron as fantastic battles were enacted, until Sheila would yell from an upstairs window, "Stop that or you'll poke out your eyes!"

Sheila Warlock ruled her nest with hard nerves. She was a small woman who did not have child-bearing hips and her prune breasts hung askance on her skeletal chest. Her husband first loved her because he was then too poor and too Catholic to seek anything else. He thought himself clever when he wooed the emaciated Sheila, for surely those hips could breed no more than one son. He discovered too late Sheila's appetite. She was as hungry as she looked. Sam gave her all that he could, and he didn't own much more than his two arms, his two legs and the clothes on his back, so he grew thinner and thinner. His young daughters' faces reflected his lean unhappy life.

When Annette, the youngest, was seven years old, he found her in the backyard, on the cold cement. She was trying to eat a picture that had been jaggedly torn from a magazine. Annette held the steaming beef casserole in her nail-bitten fingers, smelling the spicy warmth. She was incredulous when the promise of beef turned into the dull taste of paper. She chewed stubbornly until she finished almost an entire page. Sam roared when he found her. His skinny body drowned in his black suit. The tiny man, old before his time, blazed before his daughter. He stuck his finger in her mouth and made her spit out the paper. He stuck his finger so deep in her mouth that she choked and vomited. Then he rocked his little grey girl until her swollen belly numbed itself to her hunger pangs. There in the metal backyard Sam prayed to every god he knew, from the God who lived in Our Lady of Sorrows to those who skulked about the metal with cloven hooves. For a long time Annette believed that there was magic in the metal. When their fortune changed, and it did soon after, she believed more strongly.

There was a slow whirlwind churning in the backyard as the metal poured in and out. No sooner had Sam brought the scrap metal in than it was sold again. He was not shrewd but through his good nature and best intentions he managed to build a kingdom out of scrap. By the time Annette was fourteen, her hunger pangs were restricted to fast days only.

I met them in the days before salmon and blue cheese, before they became lovely. I knew them before the little cottage grew up to be a fortress; I knew and loved Annette before she turned from grey to golden. The Warlocks were strangely coloured. Their hair, skin and eyes moved and melted in the sunshine of pine and caramel to the warmth of oak and honey. When Sheila first saw me she shrieked, "Who brought that dirty Moslem into my house?"

"I'm only half Muslim," I pacified her, "and more Catholic."

My parents lived in the aloneness of an illicit passion; I lived in the loneliness of it. I had no sense of a family, for their families treated them as dead. Because my parents were ghosts, I was an uncertain child. I fell in love with the Warlocks' Sunday roasts, with their squabbles, their games, the way Sheila shouted at the girls and brushed their hair, made them breakfast and packed sandwiches and cooldrink and fruit. She tied their hair with matching bobbles and ribbons and made them polish their school shoes the night before – to keep the black Nugget off their white socks. They had huge bowls of fruit in the dining room, big shiny apples and unblemished bananas with a glazed perfection that made them look unreal. They drank milk, never coffee, and Sheila baked cakes for afternoon teas with their grandmother. Ma Sasman would look at me from the other side of the chocolate eclairs and say viciously, "The food here is not Halaal."

And Sheila would say wearily, "Just leave the child alone."

Annette brought me home and made me her sister. I was her dark twin. We echoed each other in many ways but where she was light and air, I was an ocean – mercury. We mirrored each other as the sea reflects the sky. When we faced one another, the same two braids snaked down our shoulders, the same moody eyes stared out with mournful knowing. But her sulks were wispy clouds: a toss of her hair, a stamp of her little foot. My anger was the foam breaking against the rocks, a rupture. Her anger drove her to tantrums, mine to wickedness. She found me and because it was her nature to find things, I became hers. Because it is my nature to possess, I made her mine.

We met outside Our Lady of Sorrows, the grey-bricked church. She was squinting at the sun, watching the people go by, when I sidled up to her. Sheila had sent Annette out for giggling during the sermon. She had slapped Annette's legs and told her to go outside until she pulled herself together. I had started out as Catholic that morning and then decided, when I heard the first off-key hymn, that I was feeling Muslim instead. So I prowled about the church carpark, idle.

When she took me home with her, the sisters were playing with the metal in the backyard, dressed in torn sheets and towels. Bridgette and Bronwyn, the twins, were sprawled before a jagged iron totem pole. Andrea was clanging an iron stick on a metal sheet while Chriswin blew an eerie tune on an old copper pipe. They were all chanting in their horrible tinny voices. Annette took me to Carmelita, the elder and high priestess. Annette pushed me forward and I felt the frowns of the older girls branded on my forehead. I did not know what to make of them. They looked at me with the arrogance they later became known for. Even in their poor days, the Warlock sisters were proud. There was a silence while Carmelita regarded me with a prickly blankness.

"You can be the virgin sacrifice," she said eventually.

So I became the Virgin Jessica.

Here Jessica paused in her telling. She stood up, her legs numb for want of movement. Sean looked up sharply but did not say anything. She moved stiffly to the window. It was raining, the light dim. Surely this was not the ideal light for painting? She began to feel the blood flowing in her legs again. Sean lay down his brush, told her not to peek, and made them some tea. Jessica could hear him looking in her cupboards for something to eat. His familiarity comforted her. Out of a misguided sense of politeness, Sean counted decent intervals between snacks. Whenever he visited her, he always behaved like a little boy with his schoolteacher. She looked down from her window. The road beneath was smooth with rain. But for one figure huddled into a raincoat, it was empty. The lights were on in the flats across the way. The ordinariness of this rainy Saturday afternoon made her feel that she may just be comfortable after all.

Jessica longed for Annette, for Eve. She searched for them, but Annette had slipped to her own hidden place. Jessica felt caught on a path analogous to the one she was meant to have found. Annette sent her random letters but never included a return address. Jessica wrote back and lied to her, even in letters that she couldn't send. Why could Annette not see that everything Jessica had done was out of a deep love? Sean brought the tea in pretty cups and she drank it standing. Then he positioned her on the couch and again they continued.

As the sisters drew me into their world, I started changing shape. My long wild hair was pulled and bundled with navy-blue bobbles that matched the regulation school panties Sheila bought for me. I lost my scrawny rodent features and became rounder and softer. Sheila would tell me that I no longer had that wicked look, that evil eye. I had to bite my tongue not to tell her what the neighbours thought about The Warlocks' sudden wealth and her own evil eye. She treated me as yet another of her numerous Christian duties, as if by her careless charity she could save my soul and get a better seat in Heaven. She handed out neatly packaged affection with her chunky gold-ringed fingers. Sheila seemed to think that feeding me good Catholic *bredies* would push the devil out of me. It did not though, it could not. For as much as I played the good child, I was not. I was only ever playing at being good. Like pretending that the metal was a castle and I was a princess, I pretended that I was a Warlock sister and that Jesus wanted me for a sunbeam. But I was a darkling child, I did not belong with them.

The scrap metal in the yard changed constantly because Sam was always buying and selling more. He used the backyard as a temporary storage space until he moved the scrap to the lot down the road. Then he bought more and put it back in a different arrangement, so one day the yard could be an enchanted forest, another day a magical land far above the clouds. It did not matter to us that this was Sam's work. We hardly noticed him. He haunted the edges of our world. He was like a long lean piece of scrap, waiting to be transformed into something useful. He did not take up much space and if he made any sounds, we did not listen. We would see traces of Sam rather than Sam himself. In the mornings, there would be an empty cup, a ringed coffee stain, a trail of crumbs leading from the kitchen table. At night, a hat hanging on the hook next to the door, a thin presence at the supper table which was too easily crowded out by seven daughters and a wife with hard nerves. There seemed to be almost no Sam but for the remnants of him. Even quieter, more fragile, less effective was his adoring Annette.

Annette lived in torment. Not only was she picked on by the older girls, she suffered all kinds of persecution from me. I did not want to hurt her but could not help myself. I twisted the love she had for me with the easy lies that rolled off my tongue. There were little lies, like my mother giving birth to me on a plane from the Caribbean which meant that I was not really South African and the Government could come and take me away any day now. There were demonic lies: my father beating up my mother, the diabetes that made me writhe about on the floor until she was in tears because she thought I was dying. The levels of deception I was immersed in confused what was real and what was made up. I am still not sure, for I have not become any more honest: maybe it was true, maybe my father did beat my mother; I remember very little of them. But I remember clearly the thrill I would receive from deceiving Annette. I swore her to secrecy about my supposed diabetes. I said that they would take me to hospital if anyone else knew and then she would never see me again. She cried at the thought of me dying and then sobbed at the idea of never seeing me again. I hated seeing her cry. She would stay in her bedroom, refusing to eat so that God would hear her prayers. I did not mean to hurt Annette with these stories. I told them to her because that way I knew she could inhabit my uncertain world, I wanted her to feel unsafe too. I just wanted her to be close to me.

Sometimes Sheila called me aside, crooking her thin witch finger. My blood ran cold, thinking that she would send me away. But she just whispered cryptically, "A true gentleman always sleeps on the wet spots." Then she nodded, as though she was dutifully preparing me for the future she predicted for me.

When I was fourteen, Mona came to work for the Warlocks. Mona was the sleep-in girl who slept in until ten every morning before she began cleaning. She was thinner than Sheila and quickly slipped through all hiding places and secrets. Sheila first locked Sam's drinks away, but that was no problem for Mona, whose needle fingers could pick any lock. Sheila then hid the alcohol, but the scent would draw Mona through tightly capped bottles and hidden cabinets. She listened at closed doors while the older girls whispered boy stories to each other and smoked cigarettes under the bed. Mona read diaries as part of her cleaning duties. She did not tell what she knew. Instead she gave the girls a bowl of vinegar to remove the smell of smoke from the bedroom. She once sneaked Carmelita and Chriswin in through the window when they missed their curfew and Sam was pacing in the lounge after midnight. Another time, she set their bedroom clock back so that Sam and Sheila had no idea that the two older girls were out dancing until the early hours of the morning. She did not do any of this out of the goodness of her heart: she demanded payment, sometimes in money, sometimes in clothes.

29

She would take the clothes she liked out of their wardrobes, help herself to any little trinket she fancied, and when they discovered their things missing, the older girls could do nothing. Mona had a particular way of walking. She swung her hips forward and sideways, and moved as though this momentum would keep her going. Only when they saw her swaying in their favourite pieces did they realise that Mona had taken payment. When she got tired of them, she would put the dresses and blouses back in their wardrobes with sweat rings under the armpits and smelling of parties.

I was cleverer than she was. She had her quick eyes on a bracelet that I asked Annette to give me as a token of her love. Mona hovered around the doorways when Annette and I played. She swept the yard when we used the metal to pretend we were having picnics at Kirstenbosch gardens. We had never been there and our imaginations had allowed the trees and shrubs to grow jewelled flowers. Mona sensed that there were secrets to find out but whenever she was ready to pounce, she would find a quiet Annette and an innocent me. She waited and waited but I was too clever.

Annette asked her one day, "Mona, what does rape mean?" – and Mona looked at me with glittering eyes.

"Rape is when a man stabs a woman," Mona explained. "Why do you want to know?"

"No reason," my loyal Annette said.

But Mona was persistent, so while they chewed the chocolate biscuits she had baked, she prompted again.

Guileless Annette said, "Just a story Jessica told me."

The battle lines between Mona and me were drawn. She stole the bracelet from our bedroom and then I stole it back from hers. She took it again and told me that unless I let her keep it, she would tell Annette's mommy and daddy that I was telling dirty stories. Mona knew that my position was precarious. I returned her flashing gaze and said that I would tell them that *she* was telling Annette dirty stories – after all, it was Mona who had explained rape to Annette's clean Catholic ears. Mona knew that Annette was faithful to me so she sourly put the bracelet back in my room. I was compelled to punish Annette for her disloyalty.

Jessica asked Sean for a shawl to cover her shoulders: the light was getting dimmer and keeping still made her cold. He dropped it over her shoulders. She was fond of Sean, but she wondered how much of what she had told him was the truth. She was not sure of how she felt about Annette. It changed too often. She wanted to end the story there. Sean wanted to know how she punished Annette. Jessica looked at him for a while and wondered why she was telling him this story – what was it that she wanted him to know?

"Oh I don't really remember," she laughed. "I think that my anger was punishment enough. Yes, that's what happened."

Jessica thought she sounded unconvincing and continued to explain: "Oh poor Annette, she was very upset to have angered me. Silly really, just little girls' games."

Sean was quiet as he continued painting; he had probably only half listened to what she had said.

"I have no vivid memories, no detailed or precise moments, just vague impressions and an active imagination. I have probably misremembered everything."

She was getting cross with herself for explaining too much, and she was cross that he wanted to know.

"Maybe we should stop now."

She got up and flicked on the lamps, first the big floor lamp that brightened Sean and then the other.

"You should go, I'm tired," she snapped at his big moon face. He looked injured – all he wanted was to be her best friend, just like Annette. She softened and offered him some more tea and biscuits before he left. She put them before him and said with her eyes smiling gently, "Really, there isn't anything more to tell."

He was happy again. Easy. Just like Annette.

A furious heat crept through the windows of the primrose-yellow Mercedes Benz. The brown leather seats formed a hot glue against my scrawny thighs. The sisters, three on either side of me were moist and open-mouthed, a paedophile's fantasy. Our school dresses clung to our backs as our arms and thighs clung together, sticky with sweat. The door handle jabbed into Annette's rib. We were wilting as we waited for Sheila and Sam in the hot car. The air was too thick and cross to breathe. I tried swallowing the air with fast gulps but still could not. I crawled over the sisters, pushed the door handle further into Annette's side and tumbled out of the car. Leaning against the car door, I saw a man walk into the shade of the shopping centre. He seemed familiar but I knew that I did not know him. He was wearing a light summer jacket and walked with an insolent confidence. He leaned against a pole and called out to a woman walking on the other side of the road.

"C'mon baby, light my fire," he sang teasingly. She walked on, trying to dismiss his words by pretending that she didn't hear them. A cigarette dangled out the side of his mouth. His eyes followed her and his praises shot out like poisoned arrows. He stung her with the force of his words, of his stare. This impressed me. I looked back at Annette. Her head leaned against the window and she stared ahead of her at the headrest of the front seat. Her face was passive, like a doll waiting to be picked up. I wondered what she was thinking. It did not seem that she was thinking at all.

I was thinking about that other time she had lain inert. Her face had been obscured by the barely lit dawn. Her bare backbones were hard and her head so soft against the cold cement. The grey-brown scrap hid us from the sleeping house. When I touched her, the goose-flesh pricked and crawled deeper into her skin.

The man walked further into the shadow of the shopping centre. He did not know that I was watching him. He had a silly grin on his face. He fiddled with his pants and looked around him. I got into the empty driver's seat and watched. The voices behind me were muted. Annette's foot listlessly kicked against the back of the seat. I wanted to turn around and hiss at her but I felt invisible. It seemed that to talk at all would be like clanging bells.

That cold morning, the metal had been a temple, indifferently accepting Annette's bare skin. I had an idea of how I could punish her. Rape is when a man stabs a woman, Mona had said. But what about a girl and another girl, I wondered. Did that count?

I remained still, unable to take my eyes off the man. He walked slowly across the road until he faced the wall. He placed his feet solidly on the ground, leaning back slightly as though the looming graffitied wall was pushing him down. Looking once over his shoulder, he unzipped his pants and took out his thing.

Annette kicked at the seat again. "Go and look for them, Jez," she whined. "It's too hot. I can't bear it anymore." I stayed silent.

"What's your problem?" she said rudely and then sighed, "It's too bright."

That morning, as the sun inched upwards, the yard was slowly lit. My fingers were stiff, from the cold I think. I had found a small wedge of iron so rough that it cut my palm when I closed my hand around it. It was an unclean, lacerated cut. I did not want to use my ill-fashioned knife. I felt too clumsy for that. Instead I just watched Annette as the sun slowly revealed her face. Her eyes remained shut. I touched the barest tingle of iron against her skin. We stayed there forever. I looked up at the house until, with relief, I first saw one light wink on and then another.

The man cast a furtive look to the side. His head tilted slightly as his pee trickled down the wall, down the pavement. I loved looking at his thing, I liked the way he held it. His face looked even sillier. I stared. I liked it that he did not know I was watching. The sisters' voices in the backseat were murmurs. I could see without being seen. I liked it so much.

I started drawing the line down her tummy; a thin trickle of blood appeared. I had to push hard to cut. The line curved at the bottom and then I drew the top of the J. "There," I said, "that can stand for Jessica and for Jesus."

"It's sore, Jessica," I heard Annette say.

"It's just a scratch," I comforted her. "Now you know where you belong."

Jagged streaks of blood ran from the J down her tummy. Then I saw the thin face leaning out of an upstairs window, with the white *doek* tightly knotted around her head.

"Hey!" she shouted. "Hey, what do you think you're doing?"

But by the time Mona came down to the corner of the yard, Annette was dressed and sitting up. Almost sweetly, she said, "We're just playing, Mona."

He shook his thing. His shoulders bowed. He stood bare before my unbroken gaze. I felt undescribed, untold. I was Jessica without detail.

Annette leaned over the seat. "What's so interesting that your eyes are popping big out your head?" In every sentence she spoke, one word was strongly emphasised. As she said "*big*" she breathed into my ear.

"*Sies!*" She leaned further forward. "That's disgusting. He's got his thing out. And you're watching him!"

She placed her hand on the hooter and blasted. He turned around and saw the car with girls pouring out the windows. Zipping up, he scurried off. As he left, I felt everything returning. The sisters were back with their chattering voices. Sam and Sheila were coming along in the distance carrying OK bags. I was just the Virgin Jessica in a hot car.

Like Flying

A stolen pen will bleed ink onto a thief's fingers and brand her as a cheat. She may look at you with large eyes, eyes the size of innocence, but her guilt is stained by her ink-marked hands. The blue-black bruise speaks of a black heart. They should warn you not to get too close; she scratched an officer of the Kirk, a deep, long gash on his cheek. She stole the pen after it was left on her bedside table. It should not have been put there.

In the bare room at the Kirk Hall, she did not notice the stains on her fingers. Instead, she saw the room around her, a room she knew well, and half listened to the voice of the preacher from the other side of his desk. He stood up and started moving towards her.

His smile was a slow needle advancing.

"You know we love you." His fingers barely brushed her cheek.

She could feel the smile hovering at the edges of her vision. There was concern in his voice, and she looked up, curious to see if it was real.

Leaning over to whisper, very closely and very softly – she could smell his brown teeth – he said, "Repent."

She looked at him like a supplicant in prayer.

"I have no guilt," she said.

She blocked the force of his outrage with images of fucking. She thought of hot afternoon fucking with stones digging into her back. She concentrated on the details of her yellow dress with its fine sprigs of flowers, the hair on his arms and the light inside when she shut her eyes. She remembered the one second when she had paused. It felt like forever. And then she was falling, and it felt like flying. The grass creased her skin, imprinting their leaves on her arms, her legs. As if to decipher the markings, his hands traced the cryptic pattern. Now, well thumbed – interpreted – she had been set aside.

The preacher paced the room with its scarred wooden furniture. Her eyes were Jezebel-red, for she had been questioned all night, but her skin was cast in clay. It was too late for those eyes, those lips, her bony brown fingers; he could do no more. He left her then.

The stone was not too heavy. That weight she could bear. And even though the blunt rope that bore the stone sliced into her neck, it was not the rope alone that held the stone to her back. The crowd thronged about her, but it was not them that pressed her thin shoes deeper into the mud.

The Kirk had gathered from sunrise to get a good position. They ambled about the foot of the hill, red-cheeked and watery-eyed from the wind. The brightly clad forms chatted amiably: the grown-ups reached out absent-minded hands towards their children. The grass was wet – the children could not sit down and their legs hurt from standing still for so long. They tugged at their mothers' sleeves and skirts and whined, "We want to go home." But the mothers rested firm hands on wriggling shoulders. The women talked among themselves; they talked of just desserts, of sowing and reaping and of asking for trouble.

The Kirk men hung on the outside of the circle. They did not speak of punishment. Slowly the children freed themselves. First, one escaped the hand of a mother gesturing animatedly, then another, until they all ran about in their thick-soled boots, trampling the long grass, calling with excitement. They turned round and round until they collapsed with dizziness on the wet ground. The parents trampled the muddy field at the foot of the hill with the wet weeds slapping their boots. When the rain came, the children were caught, wrapped in scarves and warm woolly hats, and bundled towards their parents. The rain did not diminish the crowd. If anything, it seemed to feed the prospect of pleasure.

At breakfast time, sandwiches were taken from picnic baskets and handed out. The women did not only look after their own. Everyone was cared for: the widowers and the unmarried men. The sun shone dully above the rain. The women, eyes squinting towards the dim glare, laughed to each other as they passed around coffee from the flasks. Their hair whipped around their faces and fingers flew out to hold back the strands. Colourful scarves blew and flowery skirts lifted gently. They caught their dresses as the wind teased, keeping one eye on their children and another more eager eye on the path emerging from the forest.

"Here she comes!"

When the shouts sounded, the women rose to their tiptoes, their necks stretched to the furthest. The children peered through and around the legs of their parents, once again restrained by the maternal hand. The husbands stared.

Tiny figures – two men and a woman – emerged from the forest and came across the wet, long grass. They set out across the field, slowly becoming bigger. The woman walked in between the men. It could have been anything, it could have been anyone: they walked in a silence that was neither companionable nor tense. The blurs switched into details – the white dress that was not a bride's and a firm hand steering her by the waist as if leading her in dance.

As she came closer, they saw her features, which confused them briefly. There was the face that was so awfully familiar, one that might be trembling in an effort to compose itself. The downcast mouth could almost be attempting to restrain itself from laughter: they had seen that many times. They would not focus on the familiar, the details that made her ordinary and loved. And the undetermined idea that she did not seem as wicked as they had remembered was cast from their minds before it was formed. They looked instead on the bride's dress that was not a bride's dress, the tired eyes, the grim preacher beside her. "How dare she," they muttered. A momentary waver threatened and they hastily fuelled against it. The cheek! The spark was lit as their indignation caught and spread.

She did not look down. She fixed her stare on an unknown point far in the distance. Her face showed no tears, her posture no remorse. The black-suited preacher – his top hat bobbing as he walked –

moved towards her and her foot moved back the barest step, her head jerking away from him. He stopped for a moment and it felt like forever. She could run now. She could turn and race across the field. She could see her hands holding the dress around her thighs, her legs spinning beneath her, and the Kirk men panting far behind. But the moment was done and the preacher was there before her. He bound her hands together in front of her.

"You have contravened the Law of the Kirk, God and Nature. Your behaviour has threatened the very tenets on which our faith rests. Husband-stealing is an assault on the Kirk, on your brothers and sisters in faith, and on love. You have abused the mysteries of the flesh as revealed in our Sacred Text." He spoke gently to her and the crowd felt deprived of a more dramatic confrontation. They had waited so long.

"Do you yet refuse to confess your sin?"

This was her last chance. The hiss of breath through bitter teeth sounded from a woman in black standing close by. But there was no pause, no hesitation, as the adulteress answered, "No," in a brave po-lite voice. She shook her head too, as if to make sure that she was understood. She walked with the preacher to the beginning of the path and the crowd pressed closely by. She waited. A man with strong hairy arms pushed up his shirtsleeves and slowly rolled a large grey stone towards them. She stared ahead. To look at him at all would crack her resolve and shame her before these people. Instead she would bear this. It would be her hysteric's slap. She hoped that pain could rewrite pleasure more effectively than silence. Her lover lifted the stone with difficulty. He held the smooth round stone against her back and wrapped a thick rope around her. She could hear the silence of the crowd as they observed them together, looking for clues to a shared intimacy. They must have been disappointed. He did not touch her more than necessary but neither did he avoid touching her at all. He was not afraid to look at her and took no special care when weaving the rope around her. There was neither dislike nor affection. If only he hated her, she thought, that would be something. She regarded those hairy arms she knew so well and watched them bind her. He twisted the rope around her back and stomach and arms, making new patterns. Her legs buckled the moment he let go. She concentrated on the pain of the burden on her back, to distract herself. She steadied herself and held out a hand to stop the preacher, who had anxiously stepped towards her. Slowly, she took a few cautious steps, and then without waiting to see if anyone was ready, she began her tedious journey up the hill. She moved slowly, like a snail making its slithery way with a stony house on its back.

Shouts of abuse followed her up the hill, shot past her and then bounced back to jeer. They called her filth; they called her a whore. She heard voices that she had heard so many times raised together in song, come together to assail her. It became its own song, the mocking cries and the catcalls. It was a sad song and the rain drummed down, and the soil beneath her feet squelched.

She wound her way up the hill and the hissing crowd followed her. She wanted to walk proudly, she wanted them to think that she felt no remorse. She did not want their pleasure augmented by her frailty. The taunts and sneers continued to rain down together with the drizzle that muddied her path. Each step she treaded was dedicated and precise but the ground was uncertain. The crowd cheered when she stumbled beneath the weight of the rock.

Closely behind her walked the woman in black. She did not leave more than two paces between them. The woman's dark dress was streaked with thick mud each time the adulteress fell. Her feet swallowed each step of the adulteress as she prayed loudly without stopping. Her cheeks were red and her mouth moved as viciously as her hands, which rubbed the beads they carried. Her face curdled as though she was chewing hard, sour sweets. The venom with which she spat her prayers hunched her body.

As the path grew shorter and steeper, the adulteress heard the woman in black panting heavily behind her. It was not the stone, nor the mob, but this that she could not bear: the strained breathing of the betrayed wife. They made their way up the tortuous path, the woman with the rock folding beneath each deep wet breath of the other. She saw the children watching her with idle interest. She saw the colourful scarves blow in the wind.

As she neared the end of her path, the shouts stopped and there seemed to be an angry silence. She had made it up the hill with too little stumbling and no tears. They felt cheated. The preacher came towards her and took the stone off her back. Her legs were barely able to hold her. He felt an immeasurable grief at seeing her almost naked without it.

The children ran about, obliviously happy. She felt weightless, as though she had left her body behind on the path and the rest of her hovered above everyone else.

From here she saw the women hold their children close and tell them, "This is what happens when you —"

This is what happens. High on the hill the wind was strong. Dresses blew wildly. Scarves flew to the edge of the cliff. Hair unravelled from tightly tied buns. The children broke free and screamed because when you ran fast enough, it felt like flying.

Like Flying II

"There is a legend in the Kumo Kirk that tells of a young woman punished for adultery," said Luke Loyola to Sean Farmer, artist and furniture repossession man.

"Of a beautiful young wife who fell in love with a married man. She was too charming, they say, far more interested in adorning herself with beads and ribbons than obeying the ways of our Word. They began a clandestine affair; different tellers say different things about how it all began. I think that it was in the Kirk Hall itself – she fainted at her grandfather's funeral. Sick with grief, she nearly fell into the grave; he had to grab her around the waist, then knees, then ankles. After that they would exchange long heavy-lidded gazes during Elias Kumo's sermons (for this was in those early days). Some say that he was besotted with her; that, driven mad with desire, he lured her away from her husband in a desperate attempt to have her for his own. Others say that she, with the help of the darker forces of nature, planted this mad desire in his loins until eventually he succumbed to her magic and fell – mostly, it is said, in the fields on the other side of the Kirk Hall.

"One day he came to his senses and found himself in the arms of the sloe-eyed hussy. He shrugged her off in disgust and rushed to seek his wife. The wife was in widow's weeds, mourning the loss of the husband she had given up as dead. There was much lamenting, until her thick black dress was soaked with his tears and he was re-united with his Kirk-blessed partner. They were ritually cleansed by the Kirk and started anew.

"The young seductress was not able to recover herself from her madness. She wrote him letter after letter, always asking him to re-turn to her, even claiming to bear his child. As for her young hus-band, I am afraid he drank himself to death.

41

"She wasted away with love, her hair grew matted, her body so thin that if there ever was a child, it too would have starved to death. (But remember, this is just a legend, we don't know exactly what is true or what was made up.) As she would not renounce her wicked ways, the Kirk had to intervene. There was not much they could do. This much we know: the Kirk authorities held a meeting and decided to punish her for her unrepentant adultery by sentencing her to death by drowning. She was to carry a millstone around her neck up a hill, and they were to toss her into the sea from there.

"She went one last time to her lover's house. His wife was at home cooking – and you understand that we have fairly complicated cooking procedures, including the sterilising of all utensils before use. The wife was busy boiling her utensils in the kitchen, about to start dinner. The young waif came into the house when the wife's back was turned and picked up the pot of boiling water. She poured this over the poor wife, who was badly scarred. They then arrested the girl and sent her to the devil by throwing her into the sea."

A stolen pen will bleed ink onto a thief's fingers. The stains will brand you as a thief. You may think you rinse the blots away but if you look closely enough you'll find that they are still there, almost invisible but sunk just beneath the skin. Your guilt is coloured by your ink-marked hands. The blue-black bruise tells of your black heart.

Jessica did not steal pens. She stole other things though: she stole cigarette lighters and umbrellas; sometimes, not often, she stole men (but she usually gave them back again); she took credit when it was not due; but most of all she stole stories. She stole stories and draped them around herself like shawls, wore them as if they were her own. She took other people's stories to keep her warm, to wrap herself in layers of history. She used these stories so that she would not have to share her own, which remained neatly tucked away beneath the stolen words. Jessica sometimes felt as though she did not experience

42

life so much as turn it into stories. Her sense of the immediate was always filtered through a voice that distanced her from events. She looked for moments to make up the most compelling story: a violin on the chair, a pair of shoes beneath it – this was an image that she kept. Standing in the bank queue, waiting in traffic – these were images that she rejected.

There were other images. Gentle water lapping, hard water knocking her over, wide blue and tiny figures on the faraway sand. An intersection where she saw remnants of glass. A childhood game with the texture of moss. A girl and her father retreating into the shadow of the mountain. Six silent sisters. But she felt increasingly trapped now – old and lonely. The present loomed too large and each second swelled. The future was too distant and the possible ends of the stories frightened her – she suspected that she was not on her way to happiness. Instead she feared that she was meant to be plucked out of the world on account of being useless; that God would realise that she did not love anyone (at least not anyone that she had spoken to in the last seven years) and that no one cared much for her, and just pluck her out. So she feared every mouthful of food: fish bones became weapons; stringy spaghetti, chewy beef at lonely lunches threatened her (if she choked, no one would hear her scream). Driving her car, she would imagine the sudden loss of consciousness, the dreadful crash of metal against metal. She listened to her heartbeat as she fell asleep, waiting to hear the irregular shriek between the regular pumps; the tap-tap of the bead curtain against glass as someone crept in through an upstairs window. She feared the bathroom, the shower, the staircase, the dark. It was not so much that she was afraid of death itself. Rather, she feared the language of death: crushed, snuffed out, passed away, dead. She found these words inadequate and misleading. They wanted to point to a contained experience, the neatly described "not here". This "not here" was disorder – it was not to be controlled by words. Her story voice allowed her to deceive herself: she could look away from the disorder and pretend that she was a character instead. Especially when there was little distinction in her mind between what was truly her experience and what wasn't. Jessica's every move was calculated to make an impression.

Sean had stumbled upon an interesting story, she thought crossly; he would stumble upon these things. She played it out in her head, added a few details, deleted the irrelevant (he went on and on about the food) and sat back in her chair.

They were to go together to the hill. Luke Loyola explained that it would be best if Sean accompanied them. This was a very private affair and the Kirk did not take kindly to outsiders. It was not real, of course, simply a re-enactment that they performed every year to mark the beginning of the Fast. They were not barbaric; nor were they outside the law. It was just a skit, a little performance so that they would remember. To mortify the flesh. Sean was only invited because he was an Artist. Because he needed to see what it was the Kumo Kirk wanted him to paint.

They set off then: Sean too tall in the back of the car, with Ana and Luke seated on either side of him. There was no room for his legs, so he parted them and placed one next to Luke, one next to Ana; her knees, tightly together, swung demurely in the opposite direction. She was lovely. Sean smelled the girlish perfume on her hand-knitted cardigan. Luke's moody coat was crumpled and smelled of empty cupboards. They were silent on the way to the hill. Sean asked a question or two but received abrupt answers from Luke, and a coquettish aversion of the eyes from Ana (she stared out of the window most of the way). The little girl, Rebecca, sat on Luke's lap, her black wellies dangling down Luke's legs, just touching Sean's trousers with their muddy tips. She wore a yellow jacket on top of her sundress, and stared at him with steady eyes. Sarah drove and Mother Loyola – a fierce, bird-like woman with steel-grey hair in a child's body – sat beside her. Sean could see the resemblance between her and Luke: they had the same bags beneath their eyes, the same haunted look. Mother Loyola (she must have been about a hundred years old) claimed not to speak any English, and he was beginning to doubt that Sarah could speak at all.

Sean had been asked the day before, when he met the Kirk leaders for lunch, to sign a confidentiality agreement. The agreement had been passed to him across the table on the veranda just before Luke told him about the legend and the ceremony. The little girl fixed her eyes on him when she thought he wasn't looking and jerked her head away when he turned to wink. Sarah, with a bent back and hard hands, clutched the back of her chair while Eben Loyola thanked God for the food. She looked about her – perplexed – and then moved in her hunched way back into the house to fetch more dishes.

Sean found Luke Loyola quite without charm – a prophet of doom and gloom. His hair was thinning and greasy, his dark clothes jarred with the summer garden lunch. As he compared the two men, a young woman, Ana, came out of the house. She looked and smelled clean and light, too light next to the preacher. He had heard the Kirk had strange sexual practices and he was keen to find out more about this. He wondered if they were odd on the side of excess or restraint. Excess, he hoped. Maybe that was why the old woman was bent out of shape. And just maybe the ritual that Luke wanted him to observe was some kinky ceremony – please God, not church.

It struck Sean as odd that he should be there at all. He would have imagined that the Kirk was on a tight budget if he hadn't seen his advance for the artwork. It had been too many months since he touched a brush and he had never been particularly good at it. It was only his vanity, an adolescent dream of glory, that made him agree to visit the Kirk after they saw one of his pictures in an old catalogue. And the money: furniture repo did not allow for too many luxuries. And perhaps the slight hope that his most secret longing might just be fulfilled.

Jessica liked this story. It reminded her of God and that made her smile. It made her like Sean more too, now that she had invented in him a sensitivity that she didn't always perceive. She wished that she had been allowed to see the Kirk people. Instead she had to rely on the details that she had greedily demanded.

45

She resolved that she would go to the Kirk, one way or another. Perhaps when Sean delivered the completed picture. Jessica liked her new story very much but it was incomplete: she had yet to insert herself.

As a stranger, Sean walked amidst the Kirk-goers. He sensed the excitement that hung densely in the air. They were bunched together at the foot of the hill, animated with delight. He saw the young girls' lovely curls and old women's crooked shoulders. The young women were neatly dressed: the unsubtle garments that barely covered too many women outside of the Kirk were unheard of here. This delicacy appealed to him.

He watched the children in their colourful Wellington boots. They ran about trampling the long grass, screeching with an excitement that seemed a discordant echo of the parents' pleasure. The chatter of the grown-ups reminded Sean of a classroom where the teacher was absent for a minute. They hugged themselves against the cold wind and stamped the ground beneath their feet.

Sandwiches were shared around breakfast time. Munching the thickly cut bread placated the children. Sean ate a sandwich with chicken mayonnaise and gherkins. He chewed happily, savouring the buttery bread, and again appreciated what the Kirk could do with food. The women laughed to each other, holding back the hair that whipped around their eyes. Their dresses lifted gently in the wind, exposing woollen stockings on some and fragments of bare leg above boots on others.

He wondered at the benign scene before him, envying them their faith. He had not thought it possible to feel such contentment at a religious ceremony. All the people seemed at ease and comfortable – as if they had known each other for a hundred years. The ties that bound them were tangible; Sean yearned for ties like these. But there was a shyness in the way the women approached the men and a reticence in the men themselves. Sean knew that the Kirk folk arranged marriages for their children, and often before they turned twenty-one. There were strict rules about sex for procreation only, but he was certain that these could not be enforced. The women looked much too happy, he thought. Besides, how would anyone know? Luke Loyola could hardly go around inspecting. He chuckled at the thought of Luke knocking on doors at night, like Wee Willie Winkie, checking that everyone was chastely in twin beds after eight o'clock.

The catcalls started just as the car emerged from the forest road. Sean felt a moment's panic at the robust reception, fearing a loud evangelical service rather than a quiet appreciation of nature. Luke Loyola seemed mild, but appearances could be deceiving.

"Here she comes!"

When the shout sounded, all eyes were trained on the car parked across the field. The women craned their necks to see; the children were momentarily subdued. The husbands just stared.

She was thrust out of the car. She wore a white dress that was too bright as she crossed the field in between the two darkly clad men. There was something about her that was familiar to Sean but he could not be sure: dark hair, dark eyes – too many women shared these features. Yet there was a familiarity that appealed to him beyond a physical recognition. As she came closer, Sean was nagged by an awareness that he couldn't quite name. Perhaps in another time, in a parallel world, they could almost be friends. The muttering around him grew in volume and in fervour.

The woman in white regarded the crowd with bewilderment. Then she fixed her stare on an unknown point far in the distance. She did not look down. A woman in black eased closer – she was maimed by a hideous burn on her cheek, a long puckering scar.

Luke Loyola in a black suit moved towards her, his top hat bobbing. Her eyes met his briefly, almost serenely, as he tied her hands together.

"You have contravened the Law of the Kirk, God and Nature. Your behaviour has threatened the very tenets on which our faith rests. Husband stealing is an assault on the Kirk, on your brothers and sisters in faith, and on love. Abusing the mysteries of the flesh transgresses and violates the Law as revealed in our Sacred Text." The harsh words were made kind as Luke Loyola spoke them. There was a tenderness in his manner that surprised Sean.

"Do you yet refuse to confess your sin?"

The crowd collectively surged forward as she breathed out a small, brave "No." They responded with an ancient knowledge; their voices roared wordlessly in tune with each other. This ritual was blue-printed deeply inside them. The crowd followed the adulteress and the preacher to the beginning of the path. She averted her eyes as a man with strong hairy arms slowly rolled a large grey stone towards them. The crowd watched in silence as the man bound the stone against her back with a thick rope. Her body held rigid, she let the man bind her without a cry or a flinch. She must have been so frightened. She held out a hand to steady herself beneath the weight. Luke Loyola stepped towards her and this annoyed Sean. Let her be, he thought as he beheld the distasteful scene before him. Enactment or not, this was a ritual in which he wanted no part. But in the same way that the stone was now secured to her back, he was bound by his curiosity. Again the crowd heaved forward: she had set out on the uphill path, moving slowly, like a snail making its slithery way with a stony house on its back.

Shouts of abuse followed her up the hill, shot past her and then bounced back to jeer. This was what most offended Sean. The clamour that arose from the crowd rang out as though it was a boxing match. He looked at the yelling people around him, their faces contorted with rage and glee. While the wind still played with the hair and dresses of the women, while they still laughed to each other, their smiles, the way they picked up the children were tinged with something sour. He watched them laugh and cheer to see the woman fall and it repulsed him. He noticed one woman with broken teeth, which reminded him of Luke Loyola. Intrigued, he found another and another and he wondered what in the Kirk's diet resulted in rotting teeth. Maybe dentistry was against their religion. Sean shuffled along with the crowd as they followed the adulteress. The scarred woman with the black dress tripped the burdened figure with an unkind foot. The crowd roared as she stumbled.

Sean searched amongst the many layers of jackets and scarves. Then he noticed a burn mark as a woman grabbed her skirt from the wind. It was a long scar of melted flesh on her leg. He found this repeated on the chest of another woman. The waving arm of a young mother was branded too. The earlier idyll had shifted. He saw the lovely Ana shake a furious fist, her brow creased into a hideous frown. Sarah's hunched form was distorted even further and Rebecca clapped her hands with uncontrolled delight. It seemed that even those who weren't physically marked were misshapen by their strange passion for the pain of others. Sean remembered his grandmother telling him that if he pulled faces, the wind would change and it would stay like that. He felt that the wild faces before him really were like that, that they had returned to their most true expression.

Sean walked behind the crowd as they jeered the woman up the hill. He could barely see her – she remained just outside of his vision. Intermittently he caught sight of her white form, now brown with mud, picking itself up. Why did he not help her? He couldn't say.

She reached the top of the path. The stone was removed from her back and, like a baby calf's, her legs slowly accustomed themselves to the new weightlessness. The cries petered out feebly. For a moment, there was a complete silence that was even more vicious than the taunts. Then they seemed to find themselves; they looked around and recognised each other from the other side of an interrupted passion. They recovered themselves: mothers pulled their children closer, others wrapped their jackets and scarves tighter as the wind blew against them. Sean wanted to cry with frustration: See, see what you have done. But then he saw women clutching their children tightly and saying, "This is what happens when you –"

The children tugged at the restraining arms. Slowly, they tried to prise themselves away.

High on the hill the wind was strong. Tightly clutched jackets strained and released; scarred skin peeked out from dresses lifting like wings. Scarves unwound themselves and slithered away. The children broke free and screamed. And their parents watched and remembered when they were young and knew what it was to feel like flying.

This wasn't quite the story Jessica had meant to find. The adulteress — who had her hair colour, her eye colour, her skin colour, her build, and a dress from her wardrobe — eluded her. But Jessica was tired and didn't feel like searching for her now. She had just walked off the end of the story (with legs like a baby calf) as if she had stepped off the cliff. Did she die? Jessica was not sure but she could not finish it now. She would try again later.

House Call

T he glass door to number fifteen was frosted and this chilled Sean whenever he inserted the key in his own lock. His door faced number fifteen in a bare brick-and-cement block of flats. Each time he stood before his door, his back to the mountain, he felt his skin prickle with goosepimples.

It was a fairly ordinary panelled door with dust heavy on the wooden frame. There was a barely discernible design etched into the frosted glass. A deep-red and gold curtain suspended behind the door veiled any further view of the flat inside. His own door held no dust and the striped glass refracted a distorted orange blob that was his couch. He had once seen inside number fifteen, when the door stood wide open with no one in sight. He was allowed a jagged angle of the flat that pieced together a royal blue couch framed by a red wall and dark, heavy drapes. He wondered at the textured rich-ness his illicit glimpse suggested.

He'd never spoken to his neighbour from number fifteen. She wore her hair long and hid behind large dark sunglasses. She smiled politely, but it was a small tight smile. He mostly saw her padding down to the garages or to the dirt bins with her black garbage bag banging on the steps. Once the bag had split open and cotton wool and leftover food spilled down the stairs. She had cursed, then stopped to collect the fruit peels, chicken bones, half-eaten rolls and take-away cartons – her hands scraping the mess together. Long plum-red nails on thin ringed fingers scooped mango-melon peels and fragile bones picked clean into empty Steers containers. He'd offered his help but she had shielded her dirt, saying it was fine. His eager eyes had scanned the contents falling down the stairs, hoping to find out who she was through what she had discarded.

Sometimes he heard her out on her balcony. He would hear the sounds of a chair scraping, or sighing as she sat down. Late at night there was the heavy groaning of the ancient pipes as she coaxed water from her taps. His room would vibrate when she turned the taps to a certain point, and the noise screamed through the building. He liked the thought of the pipes running from his flat to hers – a hidden network buried deep in the walls, forming an invisible cage that held them together. When he heard her shower spray, he would think of her behind the thin wall between them. He imagined that she could hear him and it was vaguely pleasing to him to think that they should take their showers together. But her door was cold and did not welcome him.

HOUSEHOLD APPLIANCES

Sean shut his door behind him, relieved by the warmth of the flat. They were on the third and top floor of the building, so it was always piss-hot in summer. It was a stuffy warmth with the distinct smell of a room in need of airing. He took a beer from the fridge, faxed an invoice to the furniture store, and allowed himself to feel some satisfaction at having paid the phone bill. Sean Farmer paid his way by repossessing furniture and household appliances. The company faxed him the details of the non-payments and he collected the furniture from the poor people who couldn't afford televisions and fridges. It was not pleasant work, but he did not dwell on this.

Anyway, these people often looked tired and relieved to have the burden removed from them. They could just go to another furniture store and get another free appliance for a few months, he reasoned. Others shouted at him when he arrived; or they pleaded with him: "Just till the end of the week, mister, I can get the money then, just let me see what happens on Saturday with the races. And then there is the Lotto – and you know what? I dreamt of bees plus my dead grandfather and that always means I'm getting money." Sean had learned not to listen to them, to just walk by. He was very tall and could easily carry the smaller goods on his shoulder while they yapped at his heels. Their words were lost before they reached his ears. He stored the goods in a garage under the block of flats and drove out to the store a few times a month.

It was lonely work – just him and his fax machine – and taking things away from people was not exactly enjoyable. He had not intended this; there were other things that he would rather be doing. But he didn't often think about what used to be important, and so there were no paintings on his walls.

He checked the fax machine and, relieved to find no faxes waiting, went out onto the balcony with his beer. He leaned over the edge looking at the block of flats across the way. It was a more expensive-looking block. He often watched the two balconies, to observe the movements of his neighbours. There was a man who stretched out naked at seven in the morning, his penis just hidden by the wall of the balcony, and a woman who went away for days on end. Sean wondered if – beyond his little stage – they ever talked to each other, maybe even loved each other. What happened when they were swallowed up by the balcony door: did they live tidy lives? Was all disquiet quelled beneath the hum of the washing machine, or the fridge, or the whirr of the Magimix? Did they hum along?

Today no one was home. The windows and doors were shut. He leaned over so that he could see the balcony of number fifteen. There were some thirsty plants on her balcony and a faded green deck chair. Her drying rack was covered with underwear bleached to pastel by too many washes. Like the browned leaves, they waved dryly in the breeze. No one else around, nothing else moved but the thin branches of the tree across the way. He liked having people who lived alone around him, as if they were all alone together. He swallowed beer after beer in the sun until he was officially off duty at five o'clock, when the soap operas came on.

He listened to her come home. Her heels clattered up the stairs and then paused. He heard the key inserted in the lock and the door squeak open. As she moved about inside, her heels were hard against the parquet floor and resounded through his flat. He wondered what she was doing, just walking up and down. Did she pace? Or was she doing things, useful things that needed to be done because other people were waiting for her?

He played some music, hoping she would hear and bang on the wall or something. He fried some sausage, eggs and chips, which he ate while reading *Men's Health*. He was singing in the shower when he decided to spend his evening going back for a repossession from a family who hadn't been home for several days. He was feeling rather cheerful and thought that putting in a bit of overtime wouldn't hurt. Otherwise, he would just stay in and watch TV. Frowning, he felt that the water had become cold. He opened his eyes and saw that it also had a red tinge. He shut the taps, wondering if something was wrong with the pipes. Rather that than a dead rat stuck in the tubes. The phone rang and he fell out of the shower, then cursed the thin walls of the flat when he realised that it was next door.

WHO'S THERE?

Jessica was thinking that she would not be able to bear it were it not for that tree across the way, when the phone rang. She did not know the names of flowers or plants, she could never really remember them, but she understood their textures. She loved that tree with its finger-thin leaves falling all over itself. In the evenings, she sat on her balcony and stared out at her tree against the sky, framed like a postcard by the walls of the building. She loved flowers too, but couldn't grow any herself. She reached the phone on the second ring but automatically paused until it had rung five times, her eye catching her hand resting on the receiver. Her mind was attending to half-acknowledged images: the colour of her nails, the shape of her fingers, the long leaves of her tree and the angles of her building. Immersing herself in these very ordinary details distracted her from herself, but also from the phone ringing beneath her hand. She did not remember to put on the other Jessica. Her shoes lay across the room where she had kicked them off. She stood short and unready. When she picked up, she registered the voice on the other end with mild disappointment, as though she had hoped for something she wasn't entirely aware of.

The voice belonged to a man and Jessica could not place him in any of the endlessly available categories from the quick "Hello" that he breathed into her ear. She was not ready for the silence on the other side. She spoke into the handset, her voice feeling hollow and ridiculous, unnerved by the aggressive quiet. The other Jessica would have had the sense to put the phone down immediately, thinking, what nonsense, but she was curiously suspended, unable to be sensible. So she listened to the person listening to her saying, "Hello, hello, who is this," wondering if it was a prank and feeling uneasy. The phone clicked to silence and she cursed herself. If that was a prankster dialling a random number, he had found a delicious target. That must be what he wanted, her inability to put the receiver down, being held by a stranger's voice and the silence. She was angry with herself for allowing him that. She pictured him, giggling to himself and happily dialling another random number. The other possibility she pushed from her mind; she did not want to think that perhaps this was someone who knew her. That the unknown caller perhaps had a sense of her, that he knew where she worked, what she looked like.

Music burst into her flat. It entered through the walls, the open windows and balcony door. It was loud music with not as many words as beats. The wave of discordance further unravelled her sense of calm. Jessica did not own a television or music system – instead she comforted herself on the nights she stayed in by reading thrillers. She did not like to keep still for too long. She was propelled by an unidentifiable fear. It seemed that she would be safe only if she kept moving. The seclusion of her flat hid her for a while, but she could not remain at rest. She gathered the threads of her solitary calm by running her bath water and choosing a dress. The dresses and suits hung neatly with rows of shoes beneath them.

She stood before her wardrobe, looking for a colour and fabric to suit her mood. First she tried on the green silk and then peeled it off with discomfort. She tried the short black dress which matched her moody eyes. But then she remembered who she was meeting and shrugged it off. Layers of dresses piled up on her bed, but Jessica could not find who she wanted to be that night. She bathed with oils and bubbles, then creamed and perfumed herself; slowly she was released from her disquiet.

By the time she stood before her long mirror in her red dress and high-heeled sandals, she felt fine. She drew a line above each eyelid, thinking only of the evening ahead. She coloured in her face, stretched her eyelashes and looked at herself with a raised eyebrow. Pretty. Jessica left fifteen minutes late, but she always thought it best to keep them waiting just a little bit.

STRANGE PETS

He heard her heels clacking down the stairs: almost as regular as clockwork. He looked down over the balcony ledge and saw her thin dress blowing in the wind. She held on to it with one hand, the other unlocking the garage door. It was one of those quiet, unnoticed moments, but for Sean's peeking eyes.

He tidied his supper dishes and forgot about her. He set out to collect a television and microwave from a Mr Fortuin in Grassy Park. Sean knew Grassy Park well enough. He had spent two dismal years living there while growing up.

He could not remember exactly which one of the doleful council flats was the place he had lived with his grandmother. They all looked the same to him, uniform in their ugliness. They rose out of the dry land, the monstrous offering of this defective soil. They had sprung up like weeds, but without the whimsy of those unwanted plants. The high columns dwarfed the people who lived inside them, easily sheltering hundreds. Sean imagined the flats opened up like a printer's tray, and how the inhabitants would all be huddled inside their tiny compartments, their most private moments neatly squared into the Government-recommended allowance. The roads were further narrowed by the height of the buildings that stood out like maze walls. Each block was dully identified by an alphabet letter, but the road names were flashes of an English garden. E2, Honeysuckle Avenue, Grassy Park – this was the label of Sean's experience as a maze rat, when the only flowers he knew were the sun-dulled plastic carnations in his grandmother's flat. Colour came from the graffiti on the walls and the washing that was perpetually suspended on wire outside the windows.

Even this late in the evening, Sean could see the predictably blue-collared shirts flapping in the wind. Sean's longing for colour was tantalised by the painting classes he took at the Community Arts Centre. He was inspired by the creation of colours, that it took only three to make all the rest. It showed him that he didn't need much to make more, wasn't that what Jesus said? He scratched his head. But it frustrated him that he had lived in black and white when it was so easy to make colours. He drove down the gravel roads, eyeing the teenagers wandering the streets in the twilight hours. Remembering those pleasures, he saw the café where he used to lean against the wall and smoke and call out to the girls walking by. They would play on the game machines inside the shop when they had the money, but usually they didn't.

He passed by the church hall where he had performed in countless Sunday school plays. He saw the church itself, where he had first encountered the seemingly endless ritual of kneeling and standing. He thought of the rows and rows of hard benches and thin blue cushions. His impression then of the magnitude of the church had been bound to his sense of being a son of Abraham, one of innumerable grains of sand. It was his first conscious understanding of God and remained with him still. Being one of so many, he had hoped to slip by unnoticed. Kneeling on those cushions, he had been struck by how very big the church was, how very high the sky and how it could be possible to hide in this vastness. His adult view was the disappointing image of a glorified school hall with a very big table and some rather nice candlesticks, which were bolted to the altar as they had been stolen a few times. But his childhood memory, of a magnificent and solemn resting place of God, lingered.

It was the third time that Sean had come to Mr Fortuin's house. He went once on a weekday and then on a Saturday and both times he was left with the impression that the house was not unoccupied. There was something about the thick, patterned Terylene curtains that suggested a presence hidden in the folds. He had knocked with his loud, hard-balled fist but the door would not open. A small window had been left open just a crack and the Terylene swayed sweetly. Sean was used to people pretending to be out when he came by, but this house made him feel uncomfortable. Some houses that he visited were filled with pleasant warm feelings mingled with the smell of *bredies* and others nurtured a sense of defeat, which manifested itself to Sean as the smell of too much Jik. Most times the houses just reflected a bundle of different emotions, and the presence of a furniture repossession man carried its own disturbing sorrow. There was nothing strange about the house itself, even though it filled Sean with an eerie sense of being watched. It looked much like the house next door, like most of the houses in that area, except for the bizarre built-up mix of metal and brick across the field. All that varied were the ways in which poverty revealed its decay. Two yellow squares shone out, lighting up the dry and tangled garden; the wire gate could not shut. How Sean had longed to live in one of these houses as a child. He walked to the front door and knocked.

Sean listened for the muted sound of voices, for the scuffling of feet. He strained for the monotonous hum, lifted by the occasional sound of canned laughter, of the unpaid television. He could hear none of these, yet the house felt curiously awake. He knocked at the door as he had done before and again there was no answer. Sean walked around the side of the house, hesitating only briefly at the thought of the thin, wild dogs he had seen previously. The dogs were not there – he had guessed this because there had been no avalanche of barking on his arrival. Maybe the owners were taking the dogs for a moonlight stroll. There were chickens at the back. When Sean was a child, he never met any neighbours who owned chickens – although a cock always crowed at dawn – and he regarded them as strange pets. Light beamed into the backyard from the half-open kitchen door. Just outside the door lay a garbage bag with a foul smell coming from it. He stepped over the bag into something soft.

He pushed the door and entered the kitchen. Dishes were stacked in the sink. His grandmother had taught him always to wash the dishes before leaving the house in case it burnt down while he was away. Pots and pans cluttered the surfaces. The stove was covered in a dark liquid that had boiled over; flies buzzed around the mess and a fierce stench assaulted him. In the centre of the kitchen floor was a pile of chicken feathers.

Sean tried to tell himself that there was nothing sinister about killing chickens. Just cost effective, he repeated to himself. Fetch the TV and get out of here. He walked around the feathers and stepped into the silent hallway. At the end of the passageway stood an old woman with white hair. Her hair was long and knotted and she wore an orange overall. She raised her eyes and called plaintively, "Who's there? Jessica, is that you, *my kind*? Who is that! Jessica? Jessie? It's your ma, Ma Tina. Come here, my child, come sit with your ma." Her hands fretfully tugged at her hem. She strained her neck towards Sean as though she could not see very clearly in the dim light. But her eyes – they were a startling green, shining all the way down the passage like a cat's eyes gleaming in the dark. Incandescent, Sean thought, unnerved by the apparition. He willed himself to walk forward. Instead, when the house made one of those sounds that houses make, he ran.

MANAGEABLE CHUNKS

Some people might have considered Jessica too old for casual dating, but she preferred to think of it as a complex economic system. Working as Mr Crane's personal assistant could not afford her the luxuries she so loved, but introduced her to men who could. Her currency was her attractiveness, she had plenty of that, so she invested her secretarial wages in looks and charm. The return on this included meals at good restaurants with someone to talk to instead of solitary sandwiches. This also fulfilled Jessica's most basic need, her aching to be noticed. So these dinner companions – sometimes married, she never asked, she didn't like dabbling in adultery – satisfied her vanity by attending to her and commenting on how she was the loveliest. That made her feel better. There was one subtly encroaching danger. Jessica believed that food cooked without love lacked nourishment, so she was always just a little bit hungry.

She leaned her arms across the table, thinking that it would hold her up. He was talking about clever things that bored Jessica. She disliked clever people, they used words in ways that tricked you and blurred boundaries. Cleverness was by nature devious and immoral, so she did not trust him at all. Jessica liked to think in clear shapes and angles. In manageable chunks.

The waiter interrupted his monologue and poured more wine in Jessica's glass. She was bored. She went out because she hated being by herself. But talking and eating and listening bored her. She wanted to be somewhere else, to do something else; no more wine and cigarettes and food and talk. But what else was there to do? It comforted her. It was what she knew best. Her body ached from sitting in the same position and she thought, shut up shut up, but still smiled sweetly. She thought of the too-soft kisses he would try to fire from his puckered lips and his too-soft fingers poking her shoulder bones. She thought of that peasant penis relentlessly nudge-nudging towards her, even as he spoke at her in that dreary voice. She opened her mouth to say, I must go now, but then he pushed a pretty parcel across the table. Her jewelled arms greedily reached for it – "Oh how gorgeous, is that for me?" – and she decided to stay a little longer.

JUNK MAIL

Sean lumbered up the stairs feeling stupid. He would go back the next day, he said to himself as he lifted his big, heavy legs up and down until he reached the top. And in the clear light of day, he comforted himself as the chill from number fifteen brushed his neck, everything would be fine. To be frightened by somebody's grandmother! Already the old woman had transformed into a dear little old lady. He found it difficult not to feel a sense of defeat; maybe that was why he kept his eyes to the ground, which was where he found the small square of paper. He often picked up bits of paper, eager to know where people had been and what they did. All he ever found was the easily discarded, like receipts and junk mail. But even the receipts interested him. He would skim the fine print to see what had been purchased, where and at what time, and most importantly, in what combination. He would file away the scraps of detail until he could form a character sketch pieced together from leftovers. He should have studied psychology instead of fine art. So, it was habit that made him bend for the piece of paper outside number fifteen.

There was a curious churning in his stomach when he realised that this was no receipt but the thin flowered page of a letter. He unfolded the page and read.

… to move on. If she was that unhappy, surely she would have found me by now? I do not have the strength nor goodness to pursue any sense of higher purpose. You know me well enough. You do whatever you feel necessary, I think I am done with this. Let's not allow anxiety to delude us into a false sense of affection. Nevertheless, I wish you well.

The letter was signed "Jessica". Jessica. Just as the old woman called out. This must be fate. He felt no guilt at reading the letter. He believed that anything left lying about was meant to be read, an inadvertent cry for an audience. Jessica should have been more careful if she wanted to keep secrets. He wondered if the letter was to or from his neighbour. He rather thought that she looked like a Jessica. He knocked at number fifteen and waited. She was probably out, he thought. It was just after ten and she didn't usually get home until ten thirty or later. He had just turned to his own door when the red and gold curtain swayed and a cross-looking face peeped out.

Wearily Jessica moved towards the door, ready to tell the pinched little schoolgirl from downstairs exactly what she thought of her ailing mother. The girl knocked at Jessica's door several times a month, saying, "Please can you not wear heels inside, they make my mom's headaches worse and please can you not shower twice a day, the water leaks from our ceiling and please can you not vacuum so often and do you sew? I need someone to make a dress for me." Jessica felt as though she had become the repository for all their hopes and tears. She supposed that it had something to do with living above them, that God was too far and they didn't have the energy to think any higher than one floor up. They had even presented her with a gift of ugly slippers sold on the pavement for ten rand as a way of appeasing the forces that leaked water onto clean bedspreads and kept them up at night with the grinding noise of the taps. She had never met the sick mother, only the teenage daughter with her cheap, awkward clothes, who served as an intermediary, negotiating with the higher plane. She swore that if it was the girl knocking at her door again, she would brush her hair, wipe off that hideous make-up and tell her a thing or two about wilfully wearing sacks with fake fur. But the girl from downstairs with her odd requests was the only person who ever knocked at her door. There was something binding about that. She looked through the curtain and saw the massive figure of the man next door. She groaned, thinking that the reason one moved into flats in the city was so that the neighbours didn't come knocking for cups of sugar.

"I thought you weren't home," he smiled.

BETWEEN OUR DOORS

His attention was caught behind the figure in the red dress by the richly textured room beyond. Swirls of vividly coloured materials draped the walls and windows. Sean wanted to touch. There were ornately carved statues and tapestries depicting merry frolics adorning the walls. But the flat was too small for such lush taste and the effect was a closeness that was as cloying as too much cream.

"Oh ho!" he exclaimed. "What a lot of brass! You Indian, Muslim?"

Jessica maintained her graciousness. "What was it that you were looking for?"

He turned to her and saw that she did not look quite as he had imagined her. Her eyes were too dark. He remembered the letter resting illicitly in his pocket. She writes in whispers and speaks in italics; Sean later believed that these words refrained through his mind when he first heard her speak.

"Your water okay?" he asked.

She looked bewildered.

"It's just that it was red this afternoon and I wondered if – you know – a rat or something fell into the pipes."

He could not tell if the distaste he read was directed towards him or the rat. "The water is fine, thank you." She smiled sweetly, but moved to shut the door – please will you leave now.

"Wait," he commanded, which made her eyes glitter. "One more thing," he continued in a much humbler tone. "I have something that probably belongs to you. I picked it up outside, between our doors."

THROUGH THE LOOKING GLASS

He stood before her, big and clumsy, vulnerable in his desire to speak with her. Jessica was not usually mean, but she was tired and she had been tricked by that clever man in the restaurant, so she just wanted him to leave. He was like a child fascinated by the rainbow in a prism as he stood before her door, trying to peek in to see her pretty things. Before she could think of a kind way to make him hand over what he had picked up (probably nothing more important than the cheap bauble the clever man had given her this evening), he had put one big booted foot over her threshold and she was stepping back to avoid proximity. He was commenting on the flat and loving her colours and fabrics and she was affronted because they were hers and she did not want to share them with anyone.

"I don't usually entertain visitors," she said tentatively; she was almost shy about insisting upon her privacy.

"Oh what a shame, you should, you should." He nodded appreciatively as his thick-soled boots trod over her fine rugs. He rubbed his hands together and walked around the lounge, inspecting the flat. Her place, beneath all the lavish décor, was a mirror image of his, with the built-in cupboards on the wrong side.

"What was it that you found?" she wanted to know. Jessica was possessed by an unfamiliar timidity. He dwarfed her with his height but kept his head bent and his eyes to the ground, staring at her bare feet. She backed onto the couch, as if to ward him off, and folded her legs away.

He sat down on her couch too, eyed her glass on the coffee table and said, "Mmmm, a little drink wouldn't be a bad idea. I had an awful experience this evening, climbed up all those stairs with jelly legs and a pounding heart."

Reluctantly, Jessica fetched a glass from the kitchen and served her unwelcome guest. He kept rubbing his hands together and blowing on them, like he was cold. He couldn't keep still for one moment, constantly swinging his arms or tapping his foot. He shook his knees together, then crossed and uncrossed his ankles and jingled his keys, and through all of this his tongue moved, talking, slurping, munching chips. He related his experience at the mysterious Fortuin house in Grassy Park while she listened intently.

"Man, I ran like a schoolgirl in wet panties," he laughed at himself, safely distanced from his fear. He looked up at the face of the carved statue on the mantelpiece, twisted in a perpetual grimace.

"Grassy Park, you said? I used to live in Grassy Park."

Her visitor leapt to his feet and said, "No ways, so did I!" He was overjoyed by the coincidence. "Now we have even more in common," he said happily.

"In fact, some of my family still live there," she said.

Eventually he stood up and stretched his back and put out a huge red hand like a dog raising its paw. He left then and she shut the door, relieved to see that her lounge had grown back to its normal size.

SOMETHING COMES UNDONE

Jessica loved Sunday mornings. She stayed in bed reading thrillers and eating fruit, the sticky juices spilling down her throat onto the sheets. She did not mind because she always changed them on Sundays. Then she had chocolate biscuits and coffee, the crumbs beading into the folds of her bedlinen. She did not mind that either.

That morning she awoke with a headache behind her right eye, and was cross that she should not feel well during the best hours of the week. She made her way to the kitchen, holding her eye with one hand, her other arm reaching ahead of her as if already groping for the painkillers. She moaned out loud, performing her pain even though she had no audience. It was only once she had left the kitchen that she turned and became aware of the wriggling white on the floor, like basmati rice coming to life. She noticed the trampled path, and was astounded that her skin was too thick to sense such insistent movement beneath it. Then Jessica registered the crawling mess that she had walked on and clapped her hand over her mouth because she did not know how else to respond to such horror.

She hobbled to the bathroom to wash her feet, not wanting to put them down on any of her magic carpets. Scrubbing her feet with Dettol, she fretted about how to approach the invasion. First she poisoned the maggots until her headache throbbed from the fumes, but still they would not die. They just shrunk into themselves and then stretched out again when they were ready. Jessica wondered at their consciousness. Were they aware of a threat to their lives or did they simply perceive minor discomfort? Did they want this to be their home, or were they innocent of territory and just wanted to be? She leaned closely over them as she sprayed more poison, even though she could feel it at the back of her throat. Were those little black eyes she saw? She was overcome with revulsion which ran through her body and made her leap out of the kitchen. She returned with buckets of water to drown them; this was marginally successful, but for the backwash that forced her to jump away with dread. When the water flowed away, the little maggots shook themselves dry and soldiered on. She stood in the kitchen with her nightgown raised above her legs, white corpses floating near her feet, and sobbed.

SHE SEES HER HOME IN HIS

Jessica paused before the door to number fourteen, her skin prickling with cold. She wrapped her arms around herself as she waited. She imagined how Sean would see her on the other side, her body sliced by the striped glass into a discontinuous form. He opened the door sleepily; the flat was dark and the curtains unopened. His hair was plastered to his head on the side where he had slept and his eyes were unfamiliar in this quietly domestic setting. The flat was dominated by the brown wooden cupboards and her eye was caught by the unimaginative tidiness. She recognised her own home in his; the same built-in shelves were tucked into opposite corners here. She turned to him, suddenly fearing that he misunderstood her intentions. She was conscious of her nightdress, his sleep-smelling body. But he paid no attention to this. Instead, his skin was creased on his forehead and he was concerned about her. She was surprised; she was not used to this. But she liked it, she liked it more than she would have thought. He went with her to her kitchen.

JESSICA LAUGHS QUIETLY

Sean looked out for Jessica after that. He would stop her on the stairs and chatter inanely and Jessica stopped to listen. She might move to escape, but Sean's big body was hard to slip by. He had a loud voice and a silly laugh that made her forgive him just a bit more each time she saw him. As he spoke at her relentlessly, she appreciated his plainness; she liked the way in which he sorted the world into manageable chunks. It was with something that vaguely resembled love that Jessica came to regard Sean. Not love as she understood it, not the love that she avoided, but a certain familiarity and comfort in the ordinariness of another person. It was certain in that it was neither grand nor illusive, just a steadily plodding knowing. His large, awkward hands, the face that exploded into teeth, his drearily clear eyes – all of these repelled her still. She did not want to touch his hulking shoulders, but she liked looking at them. She liked having them near her. And she did not mind too much when he came to visit, she did not mind because he filled the room with his burly body and laughed loudly, from deep in his belly.

The Moss Garden

*T*ired? Lonely? Depressed? Abandoned? No money? Marriage troubles? Unloved? Legal problems? Low sex drive? Impotent? *If you have bad luck – divorce, sickness, no home, no work, no food, curses, ghosts, theft, crime, rape, loss of hair, evil spirits, heart disease, kidney, liver, teeth, skin lightning, eczema, warts, boils, change of life, pregnancy, infertility, lottery, bad dreams, miscarriages, low self-esteem, suicide, car trouble, no car, memory loss, circumcision, virginity testing and preserving, virility, insect invasions – WE CAN HELP YOU! Dr Ishmael Gordon (BA, MPhil, DLitt, DipHom) has returned to Cape Town after an intensive training period with John Two Trees Romero. He has spoken with Nature and learnt the Secret Way of the Masters. He has journeyed to the East and achieved Enlightenment. He has cured thousands all over the world. Dr Gordon wants to help you. He has found the New Way. There is no need for suffering and tears. Open yourself to the healing powers of Dr Gordon and find the path to Fulfilment and Peace. Heal your soul. Commune with Nature and the Stars. You are a Child of the Universe. Also improve your finances, career, love and looks. For corporate functions, Dr Gordon is available to walk on hot coals.*

That day Evie walked. She walked without knowing why she walked – just longing to feel her legs moving, her heart pumping a bit faster. She walked because she was tired of being still. She walked because she wanted to walk alone.

On a hill near the sea is the old stone house where Evie lives with Stephen. Every night as she falls asleep in the upstairs room, she hears the sea and it comforts her. The roof slants down on either side of Evie like an upside-down boat and the beams hang low above her bed. In winter the rain strikes down and Evie feels as though she is afloat in a tin bucket. In summer the house fills with thin-legged hopping insects, but Evie has learnt to abide. Her upstairs room is so cold that even this late in summer she is covered by sheets and blankets. Her chest tightens because of the damp and her sleep is disturbed by a cough which falls into a rhythm with the waves crashing outside. There is an unwashed pine chest of drawers next to her bed. Behind the drawers, the wall paint is scarred with rising damp. The view from her window, from her bed, is of pure sky. Her wrist hangs off the edge of the bed, her fingers are spread. She wakes now, she is thirsty, her head turns with the mild bewilderment of waking. She slips her legs over the side of the bed, but the floors are stone and her stomach cramps from the cold.

Stephen is asleep downstairs. He does not hear her moving about and does not feel the damp as Evie does. He sleeps evenly, with light snores and no tossing – his body is a mound beneath the green covers, no face, just a bit of hair at the top. Years later, just after Evie leaves him, that's how she remembers him; that's how she thinks of him in the mornings.

Shivering, Evie moves back to her wooden bed – a flash of pale against the dark room – and turns about, unhappily diving into her pillows like an anxious swimmer until she eventually falls asleep.

Evie often dreams the same dreams. She doesn't know very many things.

In the morning she wakes up to Stephen bending over her.

"Your cough was bad last night," he says, holding out her slippers. She glides her feet into the slippers – she dislikes them because they are pink and feathery with a little princess heel – and holds out her arms as he helps her into her dressing gown. Evie kisses him good morning and they walk together down the stairs.

Stephen has made toast and tea. Evie likes her tea black in the morning, with lots of sugar. They eat their toast in the kitchen. Evie is perched on the high chair at the kitchen counter, spreading honey on the buttered toast with bacon while paging through a magazine. Stephen sits down with his newspaper and his morning cigarette –

his hands fidget and cannot keep still. They don't talk very much, just some trifling comments about the crime, the wind, the grocery shopping. He cleans the breakfast dishes while Evie washes. She is downstairs, dressed and packing her bag, by the time he drives off to the office in his little car.

Evie goes to the beach and reads a bit from her book in the shade of a rock. She always sees the old woman with the shrivelled skin and black teeth. Evie wonders if she is shrivelled from an hour in the water every day or from age. The woman waves and strolls away – she has a chameleon walk, wavering yet steady – with her dogs running ahead. When it rains lightly, they are the only people who come to the beach. Evie does not know if the old woman comes in the heavy rain – she stays at home and looks out the window on those days. Evie sketches the rocks, but she is not very good. Her rocks and sea stay at the front of the page, she cannot make them go back a bit. She scratches the fine fibres of the paper as she tries to push them further into the distance. She looks up at the sea skipping coyly before her. It is so dense; she is sure that a little further in (where the mermaids hide) it is firm enough to walk on. But Evie thinks that she is afraid of the water because Stephen has told her that she should be. He says that she nearly drowned once. She can't remember this; she stands at the edge of the sea and feels the fresh cold against her toes.

At lunchtime she returns to the house to meet Stephen. He comes home for lunch, even though the drive is long, and makes sandwiches and salad for them. He tells her about his morning, saying, "It's all so very tedious, sweetheart, you wouldn't understand." He asks her what she's been doing and she tells him that she spent the morning drawing. He looks at the rocks and declares the picture beautiful. The sea is behind the rocks, almost invisible.

In the afternoon, when Stephen has gone back to work, Reza comes by. They go to the upstairs room and talk and love. Evie is happy when he visits. The room is not so cold because the afternoon sun brightens it, making the pine furniture shine orange. She runs her hands over his young body, liking the feel of flesh and smooth skin. Reza's skin is as black as magic and soft to touch. Evie touches and absorbs all of the warmth and lightness she finds there. Then Reza must leave before Stephen comes home. She dusts the bed to empty it of Reza's Indian-black hairs. She thinks of her hands on slick skin-covered bones: his back is grooved and dented, the skin pulled tight. She thinks of her hands resting in the valley of his back and it comforts her. She falls asleep with the stray strands loose in her hands.

She wakes up with Stephen bringing her tea and biscuits. He leaves the tea, milky with no sugar, and goes down to prepare supper. An hour later he comes to fetch her. She is lying on her bed, not thinking, and they go down to eat. It sometimes seems to Evie that they are always eating. Stephen stands above her at the dining table with embroidered linen (Stephen likes embroidered linen), bearing a tray of food. He is anxious that she finishes her food, that she does not slice and fold it into itself.

"What is wrong with the food, my love, does it not taste good? Can I fix you something else? Have you been eating sweets again? You must eat properly, you know, or else – ".

He looks so old and tired. She wants to smooth away the lines next to his eyes. She eats her food because she loves him so.

Evie is wearing a long summer dress that once belonged to someone else. She remembers the wearer of the dress turning a corner, the patterned edge just visible. But the memory is barely perceptible, just out of reach, like the figure just turning the corner.

After supper, they walk in the moss garden. They will try to find the path tonight on the hill behind the house. Last week, they found it in the wind on the beach. The path is tangled but many walks have cleared a thin vein of sand and stone. Evie places her feet carefully so that they don't twist over the uneven edges of the stones. Stephen walks ahead; Evie watches his back bob as he threads their way into the garden. His shirt is damp where his shoulder blades meet.

For as long as she can remember, Evie has walked the moss garden with Stephen. He has always told her of the fragile garden where moss grows in wild abundance and exists in the magic hours – twilight, midnight and dawn. They don't always find the garden, sometimes they just walk and walk in the cool quiet evening; they don't even need to walk – occasionally, it comes to them when they are quietly inside.

Stephen told her: "In our fragile garden, and it is ours alone, we can't think of bad things. It will stay hidden if we threaten it with bad thoughts. You know that no sadness or sorrow is allowed here."

So Evie has learned not to think about sadness or loss. She has learned so well that all her memories are happy thoughts of Stephen and their cosy home.

They would start their walks in the forest or on the mountain or the beach and gradually they would feel the garden getting closer. The air would be sharper and Evie, out of breath, would find traces of moss. She would feel strong yet calm and the serenity could sometimes lull her into asking the forbidden questions. Once, they were nearly there when she saw some Cape may growing.

"We should pick some for Mommy," she said. As soon as the words were out she clapped her hand over her mouth; but it was too late.

Stephen turned to her sadly: "You know what you've done, don't you?"

She nodded.

"What have you done?" he asked patiently.

"I've spoken about bad things, so we won't be able to find the garden tonight."

And the lightness would disappear, the air would be dull again. They had to turn around and move back to the house, Evie feeling a weight on her shoulders because she had disappointed Stephen. He did not speak to her again that night. He never does when she disappoints him.

As they walk, they find a green patch and here Stephen kisses Evie and undresses her. Slowly he lays her down and loves her the way he always has in their moss garden.

On the day that Evie walks, Stephen leaves for work as usual, kisses her as usual and tells her not to eat too many sweets. She sets out for the beach and when she gets there, she walks on. She does not feel defiant, she just feels like walking. She walks to the bakery where she and Stephen have their Sunday morning croissants and buys a big sticky cinnamon bun. She eats this as she walks and wipes her cinnamon hands on her dress. She walks by all the tourist shops with their bells and shells. Even though they look so pretty, she walks past without entering because Stephen says that they are dishonest. She feels calm and controlled, as if she is going somewhere, except that she has no idea where. The day is warm and the wind mild, but presently she feels her dress cling to her armpits. Her hair is heavy and makes her back sweaty, so she bundles it on top of her head. She carries on, her sandal strap beginning to chafe. She follows the railway line. The sea is moving away from her, it is not quite so close to the road anymore. Then, with an unexpected fizzle, her sense of purpose leaves her. She is hot and her legs are tired from walking. She wonders whether she should turn back, and then sees a train in the station, the doors wide open. Evie decides quickly: she runs and jumps on just as the doors slam together, catching her back. She is breathing loudly and her face is shiny. There are not many people on the train, just some ladies wearing straw hats and checked shirts, reading library books. She plonks herself on a seat and sees too late the darker blue outline of the previous occupant. She avoids leaning her head back on the headrest with the shiny patch. Her mouth is dry with thirst and she licks her lips; her spit is thick and not enough. The woman across is drinking ginger beer and Evie cannot bear to watch her delicately greedy slurps.

Evie shuts her eyes, soothed by the regular beat of the train. They flicker open and she watches the electric cables run against the sky. Her eyes shut and her head falls back against the shiny patch, making her jerk forward and open her eyes again. She leans her elbows against the window and looks out. The sea has followed a different path and she sees dry, dry grass. Her eyes close again.

73

She awakes to find rows of houses flying past the window. Alarmed, she tries to decipher the landscape, then perceives a man standing next to her, bored. The woman with the ginger beer is gone. He is looking at her, waiting for her to do or say something. He is in uniform and this makes her feel safe.

"I think I am lost, mister, can you tell me what place is this?" She gestures to the flying houses.

"Your ticket, lady."

He speaks in a loud bored voice. She remembers too late the ticket. She repeats, "My ticket?" and his eyes catch a little light.

"Your ticket, lady. You cannot ride on this train without a ticket."

"Can I buy one?" she lifts her leather purse that hangs around her neck.

"No, you may not buy one. It is too late to buy one. You should have bought one before you put your foot on this train."

He writes out a fine of fifty rand and pushes it towards her. Evie only has fifty rand in her purse and she does not want to spend it all on the train. She might need it. So, feeling uncomfortable, she tells a lie. She says, "I don't have that much."

The man in the uniform pulls her arm. It hurts but she is embarrassed and does not want to draw attention to herself. She stands with him at the door; the window is half-open and she feels the wind hit her face, her hair flies back and the wheels sound loud against the track. They slow down. Evie sees a platform with lots of people standing expectantly: the train has arrived. The few cement benches are occupied. People are pushing against each other to get on the train. Evie floats by them and the train stops before a few people on the far side. He pushes her out of the train. She is off-balance when she stumbles onto the platform, and he smiles grimly, calling, "Careful now."

She is in Mowbray. It says so in big black letters on the yellow board. She doesn't think that she has ever been to Mowbray before and tries to place it on the line to Cape Town. Evie is not stupid, so she goes to the ticket office and asks about the next train to

Simon's Town. Then she asks how far it is to Rondebosch; that's where Stephen works. The ticket man is friendly: he smiles at her and tells her that it is not far, much much nearer than Simon's Town, she can even walk there. "Just follow the road," he says.

It is hot outside the station, there is no sea breeze to cool the air. Instead, there are too many people thronging about; everyone is coming and going. She hears the sound of trains and their whistles; the taxis are unloading and loading and then driving off again, the buses are slow but big and wobbly and take up so much space. People are rushing about, moving from taxi to train. She sees women selling fruit on the side of the road. She buys some deep-red plums and rests against the railing to eat them while everyone around her seems so frenzied. The plums are sweet, the skin tight and tasty. The juice squirts over her dress as she bites into them. They are warm from the sun and sweat inside the plastic bag. There is a sticky stain on her dress, browned by the specks of cinnamon. She steps into the road and forgets to look for cars, so an oncoming taxi just misses her as she jumps back. The driver swears and spits on the ground next to her. Then another taxi is standing next to her, the driver saying, "Hey lady, are you okay?" And Evie wants to cry because no one has ever spat on the ground next to her feet. She nods, bewildered, and crosses the road to find Stephen.

I'm just a little girl, she thinks to herself.

The pavement is dirty; the buildings are old and pretty but so very dirty, and there are too many smells. Evie moves away from the station into one of the side roads where there is more shade and fewer people. There is a fish shop on the corner with a butchery next door. She looks at the chunks of pink flesh cushioned by white fat in the window and thinks of the lamb chops Stephen cooked the night before. She sees whole dead fish, with eyes staring at the side of the glass cabinet. She passes a paint shop, a dry cleaner's and a hairdresser and her nose burns from all the smells that come at her. Some people are crouching in the shade. She wonders what they're doing, just sitting there like that. There are many vendors in the heat on the side of the road selling sunglasses, bags, cigarettes, second-hand curtains, dirty old coats and jackets (in this weather? Evie thinks, wiping her forehead), curry spices, toys, wild herbs, clothes. Evie goes over to look at the things. She likes the sunglasses but they are melting from the sun, the bags have a greasy sheen from sweaty fingers touching. The fruit is beginning to smell just a bit too ripe. The owners look too hot to care. She asks a vendor, "Is it always this hot here?" And he shakes his head.

"It's the end of the world," he tells her. "I've never felt the sun this strong."

Evie walks on. "Just follow the road," the ticket man said. A child thrusts a pamphlet at her. He is wearing a tattered green track top that says "Princeton University" and has a crust of snot around his nose. Another half-remembered image rises but recedes too quickly. Poor thing, she thinks, he will never go to Princeton University. She takes the pamphlet and is about to crumple it onto the pavement with all the other wrappings and flyers, when some words catch her eye. She reads, and the world slows down. She feels as though Dr Gordon is talking to her, that he alone feels her sorrows, that he alone can heal her. His address is here in Mowbray. She looks at the name of the street she is in: Hare Street. That is Dr Gordon's road. This must be fate, she thinks. Around her, no one else stops, only Evie and the boy are at rest. The boy's arm extends lethargically to the passers-by to share out one thousand flyers.

Evie walks down the street. The houses are hidden behind electric gates and barbed wire. They are pretty little cottages and too humble for such elaborate defence. She walks until she sees the red painted sign that lists the maladies Dr Gordon promises to cure. Outside the cottage some worn-looking people are sitting. *Bergies*. Stephen has told Evie not to look at them, to pretend they aren't there. But they are oblivious to her. They sit together and have no interest in Evie. She says, "Excuse me, please," because they are blocking the entrance, and a man asks her if she has any skin lotion. The woman is not wearing a bra and Evie can see her nipples poking through her dress. Her breasts look heavy and sore, dangling like that. Evie's eyes linger too long: the woman raises an angrily pointed finger and a shrill noise escapes her throat. Just in time, Evie slips through the gate and walks up the garden path. The door is open but the security gate is locked. Evie rings the bell and a plump woman with lots of big heavy jewellery comes to unlock the gate.

"Sweetie, you really shouldn't walk around with your purse around your neck like that. It's not safe. These *skollies* will grab it. Put it under your dress, under, yes like that. Now that's better."

The purse is heavy and uncomfortable between her breasts. She feels it there, too big, like a witch's third tit suspended from her neck. It's bigger than her breasts. But Sonya, as the woman introduces herself, has huge boobs that can nestle things, so she couldn't know Evie's discomfort.

"I am looking for Dr Gordon," she says, her voice soft with shyness. She is ashamed to admit that she needs healing. But Sonya cocks her head to the side and looks at her with lizard eyes.

"Many people are looking for Dr Gordon without even knowing it." Her head has an almost imperceptible wobble. "Thank God you've found him."

Sonya holds out a plump arm that jingles with bangles. Her skin is freckled and her hair, beneath her straw hat, is raggedly cut and orange. "Come now, the doctor will see you when he can."

Sonya fusses about like an old lady. Her feet are bare and dirty, her old Indian-print frock torn. But Evie likes the way she jingles; she follows the jingles into the waiting room, where the plagued patiently kill time before they are healed.

The room is cool and dirty white with crystals, buddhas, angels, and other fierce-looking creatures standing guard. The people waiting inside are creased and forlorn. Evie hopes that she does not look like that. But her dress is stained with fruit and cinnamon and there are rings of sweat beneath her armpits. She takes a number, twelve, and sits down on a wooden bench to wait. The man next to her is watery-eyed and coughing. His cough comes from deep in his lungs and he doesn't cover his mouth. The woman on the other side of her is smoking a cigarette. She stares distantly ahead and the smoke wafts over Evie. She has a child on the other side of her, wearing big shoes and kicking against the bench, repeating endlessly: "Two little dickie birds sitting in a tree, one called Peter, the other called Paul, fly away Peter, fly away Paul . . ." Her blonde Barbie walks in time to the recitation, up and down the arm of the bench, going nowhere. The mother just stares at the wall on the other side of the room.

Evie picks up a magazine and looks at the pictures of skinny models in trendy clothes. They look hungry. She reads the agony column and feels so sorry for these people with their miserable lives. She reads the letters and shakes her head in disagreement. She looks at the star gossip pages and wonders who cares. She looks up and sees that there are no fewer people in the room. The bench is getting hard beneath her. She picks up another magazine. The child is still repeating her recitation, Barbie is hopping like a bird and the miniature platform shoe continues to thud thud against the bench. A faint smell of urine becomes slowly more persistent. Evie hopes that it is not her. She looks at the coughing man and he gets up, shuffles with a bent head to the toilets. Her back hurts from the bench. When the coughing man shuffles back to the bench, he sits closer to her.

"Haven't I seen you here before?" He leans to her, his mouth wet with spit.

"Oh no, this is my first time."

"Your first time, huh? Tell me, what is your name?"

Evie tells him, worried that Stephen would not approve of her talking to strange men. Stephen! She forgot that she was on her way to meet him before he went home for lunch. It is too late for that now, he will be at home already and see that she is not there and he will be anxious and furious. He will go to the beach to look for her and find that no one has seen her all day. Evie does not know what to do. She has already waited an hour. She imagines

Stephen sick with worry, not going back to work until he finds her. Reza will sneak in through the window and Stephen will know that she is sharing the moss garden with him. The man leans in closer.

"Don't you have a ten rand for me man? My brother died last week and now it's his funeral and I don't have anything for flowers. Not a cent. Please man. Just a ten rand or whatever you can give."

Evie stands up to leave. She looks at the people around her and is filled with such an intense longing to see Dr Gordon that it paralyses her. If she goes home now, she will never see Dr Gordon, Stephen will never let her. "I'm sorry," Evie mumbles, "I don't have any money to give." Stephen has forbidden it. She sits down again. Dr Gordon's promises echo in her head and somehow Stephen's disappointment can't reach her here.

The man is talking away, telling Evie, who is not listening, about his troubles and how Dr Gordon gave him herbs that helped chase the devils away. She does not want to hear about his devils. She nods at him every few seconds. She is very good at pretending to be interested while withdrawing into her own thoughts. Then Sonya comes to fetch the man with devils because Dr Gordon is ready to see him.

The child continues to chase away, call back Peter and Paul, but now she is mixing the words and saying, "Two little dickie birds sitting in a tree, k-i-s-s-i-n-g," and somehow, Peter and Paul end up with a baby carriage. Barbie is now kissing the bench. The mother is smoking another cigarette. Barbie and the bench are getting more and more intimate and the girl is making sound effects. The mother looks down at Barbie having sex with the bench and grabs her out of the girl's hands. She hits her daughter with Barbie, the breasts against her arm. Barbie makes a whooshing noise as she comes down on the child. There are red welts on the little girl's arm and her face screws up and she screams her pain. The mother picks up the child, her arm pushing her daughter's dress above her knickers. They leave the waiting room and as they reach the passage the mother starts ranting at the child, until Sonya's loud voice drowns them both.

Sonya is trying to soothe the child but only succeeds in making her scream at the top of her voice.

Sonya comes to Evie with a red face, her nod-nodding head and fixed smile making her look like a scary toy.

"Dr Gordon can see you now," she says, out of breath. "What terrible energy those people have." She shudders as she says this. Evie gets up and wipes her hands on her dress. She wishes she had gone to the toilet first. Evie tucks her hair behind her ears and follows Sonya nervously. Sonya leads her down a long passage. The doors are shut. Just as they reach the end, they turn left into the consulting room. Sonya opens the door, Evie enters and the door shuts with Sonya outside.

Evie looks around the consulting room. The walls are lined with shelves bearing dry animal bones. Padlocked glass cabinets hold tubes and jars containing leaves and powders. She hears a voice from behind her.

"This room is auspiciously positioned for healing."

She turns to see Dr Gordon. He is wearing a white coat, as doctors do, and has sad green eyes. She feels him looking into her soul, he is so beautiful. He looks long and hard into her eyes.

"You are not well," he says after a silence. "I can see it by the dullness of your eyes."

Evie's heart leaps at his diagnosis. She is glad she stayed, prepared to pay whatever it costs. She realises suddenly that she doesn't know how much that will be. He sees the shadow pass her face and asks in that gentle bedside voice, "What is wrong?"

Evie's eyes burn, her throat hurts and she fears that she may cry. She wants to tell him everything that is wrong, that she cannot remember whole years, that there are so many things out of place. Instead she says, "I don't think I have enough money. I only just realised that now."

Dr Gordon asks her how much she has and says, "Hmmm, that is not quite enough. Who knows what extras you may need. And don't forget the medication."

She has waited so long, she thinks, almost all her life.

Dr Gordon smiles at her and says, "Don't worry." That cool peppermint voice – Evie can feel her worry seep away. "I am sure that we can arrange something."

"Anything," she says. "Whatever it costs, my father can send you the money, he has lots."

"Anything?"

She sits on the bed. He presses cold equipment against her back and listens to her breathe. He puts a stick into her mouth, presses it about and says, "Good, good." He asks her questions about where it hurts and why and she begins to tell him about all the things she cannot speak of in the moss garden with Stephen. And as she speaks, she can feel the presence of people who have hovered in the shadows for years. It seems that she might remember, they are so close. But then Dr Gordon stops asking questions and tells her to pee into a jar. She goes into the cubicle in the corner of the office. She has too much pee, it continues after she has filled the jar and splashes all over her fingers. There is no place to wash, so she wipes her hands on her dress. She is shy when she returns to the beautiful doctor with dirty fingers and a cup of pee. He pours some powder into her pee and leaves the colour to change slowly. He tells her to unbutton her dress so that he can smear ointment onto her chest. She lays herself down on the bed, wishing that the doctor had covered it with a fresh towel first. Who knows what germs might lurk there? He smears the ointment on her chest, his hands flitting across her breasts. He listens to her heartbeat with the cold equipment and then pushes it aside, saying, "I can't hear anything." He puts his hand, palm flat, beneath her breast and puts his head down to listen. He stays like that for a minute; his head is heavy. Then he moves her smaller hand with his to feel her own heartbeat. "Most irregular. Can you hear? It's leaping about, this is clearly a case of heartache."

He massages her heart with more ointment and she can feel his hands smoothing away the bumps. His hands are rubbing her breasts now and he smiles at her. He smears the ointment with the green minty smell on her tummy and turns to look at her pee which has now turned bright blue.

"Just as I thought. Your troubles are caused by lower chakra problems."

He takes another ointment from his cabinet and continues to rub her tummy.

"Can you feel that? And that? These are all energy points. It's good that you came, my girl, because you would have been in such trouble otherwise. Such trouble." He shakes his head to show how grave it could have been. He continues to rub her energy points. He slips his hand in her panties, saying, "The lower I go, the closer I am to the source of the bad vibrations, so the effect is more potent."

She can feel it, as his magic fingers move lower and lower: she can feel a stirring in her energy fields.

"The healing process takes time. You will need to return for more treatment."

Evie nods. She can feel her lower chakra quivering.

As Evie dresses to leave, he says, looking at some powders in the cabinet, "You must come again. There is much healing to be done. I've hardly even begun treating your problems. You can give your fifty rand to Sonya on your way out."

When she sees her at the desk, Sonya leaps forward to hug Evie. "You look wonderful, you're positively glowing, my darling. Isn't he fantastic?" Sonya lifts a finger to show a big sparkly ring. "Aren't I lucky? We have shared many lives together, I know it down here," she places her hands on her stomach. "You're coming again then? Wonderful."

As Evie steps into the street the sun is at four o'clock and less bright. The woman she saw earlier is stretched out asleep on the pavement, ringed by fallen hibiscus flowers, some bright pink, some decayed. The others have left. She goes back to the station and waits for the train on the poor side. All the way home she is on guard for men in uniform, for she has learnt not to trust them.

Stephen sits at the window waiting for Evie. She sees him there, leaning his head on his hands the way he tells her not to. He looks up when he hears the gate squeak open and stares at her through the window as though she is a ghost. She reaches the front door at the same time he does and she sees that he has been crying. He pulls her very tightly to him; he smells of cigarettes. He fusses about her, wants to fetch her tea, but his hands are shaking and he walks in circles, saying, "Oh Jesus, oh thank Jesus."

"You poor thing," she reaches out to stop him, "you poor, poor thing. Did you think that I was not coming back?"

He nods, hands shaking. "I thought that they had fetched you and taken you away from me."

She boils the kettle to make tea.

"I won't leave you," she promises, intent on crunching chocolate biscuits – she is ravenous.

After supper, Evie props him on the couch in the lounge and says that they should rather not go walking, he is not well. She offers to read him a story instead. Evie curls up on the floor next to the couch and he strokes her hair fondly. She is reaching for her bag to take out the book when Stephen speaks.

"Something happened today."

"Tell me."

"While I was waiting here for you, someone climbed through a window into the house. He didn't realise that I was here."

Evie looks at him with shocked eyes and says, "What happened?"

"I chased him away. Told him never to set his filthy hooligan feet in my house again."

"Were you frightened?"

"A bit."

"Did he seem dangerous?"

"The strange thing is that he didn't look too much like a hooligan, he seemed quite normal – I mean, like us. Maybe he was looking for drug money. Little brat."

"Do you think he could have hurt you?"

"Don't you worry about me."

"I think that he could have hurt you." She nods her head. "I know it."

"He was too slight. He couldn't possibly have hit me."

"That's not what I mean."

He kisses the top of her head. Evie pulls her book out of her bag and Dr Gordon's flyer falls out.

"What's that?" Stephen's feeble voice and feeble eyes are quick.

"Just a flyer a child on the road handed to me, it's nothing."

Stephen dangles his weak hand in front of her and Evie gives the flyer to him.

"You shouldn't read while lying down, it's bad for your eyes."

"Ha," he snorts as he reads the pamphlet. "What rot. And some poor buggers will believe this nonsense. Humph! If he was that enlightened, he would be reading the corns on toes in Constantia, not looking at warts in Mowbray. Utter nonsense, all of it. What do you think, Evie?"

Evie looks up at Stephen, wraps her arms around his legs – she adores him so – and says, "Yes, you're absolutely right, utter nonsense, all of it."

Stephen settles contentedly on the couch. He is smiling and his eyes are closed, and Evie's quiet voice comforts him as she reads him her story.

Nightwatch

She found him out through what he was not. She was told that he was not tall, not thick, not dark and not young. She did not know how she could possibly know him if he was only a bundle of nots. And she grew to know him in his absence. She knew him best when he was not there.

He came to her first as a voice. A slow voice – not fast, not deep – a voice that had no body. She would hear this voice in the quiet hours of the morning. At three o'clock on the community radio station he would speak to her but not to her. A train went by at this time every morning, a quick rumbling sound. She wondered where it came from, who was on it. At the same time – just audible beneath the distant clamour – the radio presenter would say, "And now for some words of inspiration from Luke Loyola."

She liked the sound of his name. The Ls would wash over her mildly after the quickly rumbling train. She came to own these sounds – the train and the lulling name of Luke Loyola. He spoke quietly. He said no prayers and did not speak of God, yet every word was a prayer, was the name of God. Or so she thought.

She thought too much there in the dark, closed-up theatre. There was not much else to do. Even when the building was active, there was not much to do but stand and watch. This was all right for her, she liked watching. But when everyone left and the building was hers alone, there was nothing to watch but the still brick walls. Or worse – the possibility of a presence. Alone at night, while on guard in the dimly lit theatre, she sometimes felt as though the building was watching her. The great brick walls, the glass windows that yielded no light but only reflected the rough brick and dark irregular corners, made her quite uneasy. It was a theatre after all, and there remained that furtive bond between performer and spectator.

Alice seemed a caricature in her too-big uniform. She played the same role almost every night and had all her movements marked out for her. She had no lines because she was a marginal character, an extra whose presence was necessary, but only so far as it enhanced the mood. With her cap pulled low over her eyes and her hair bundled up, there was nothing to distinguish her from any other guard playing that role. And if the building was watching her, it was an indifferent gaze that simply marked the movement of a uniformed figure repeatedly performing an arbitrarily chosen sequence around the building. Alice performed her part with the same shyness that accompanied her vigil when others were around. Perhaps that was why she made a good guard: she skulked in the shadows with thieves and cockroaches.

Alice dimmed the lights. It was disarming to emerge into the now shadowed building: the theatre was unthreatening until it hid its corners. There were still some stragglers in the bar, the light catching them, part shaded, part pronounced. Alice felt both comforted by and resentful of them. A woman remained tightly perched on her stool, leaning forward to talk intimately. She was Jessica Warlock, personal assistant to the director. Alice watched Jessica. She often watched Jessica, who spent many late nights in the bar. Her high heels were hooked on the steel rung of the stool and held her steady. She flapped her hands threateningly rather than flirtatiously and cackled when she should giggle. Her partner's mouth loosely dangled a fag, which stayed there like a careless comma even as he spoke. The barman offered last rounds and surreptitiously passed a double whisky to Alice. The music students, decorated with their instruments, the couple at the corner table – all seemed oblivious to her presence. The security uniform blotted her out like a magic cloak.

Alice downed her whisky and turned to see the couple sway out of the bar. The man wrapped his arm around Jessica, his fingers trailing around her waist. The high heels wobbled.

A burst of wild laughter made Alice turn to the students. There was always laughter; she seemed to move on the edges of other people's laughter. She drew out her cigarettes and leaned against the entrance to the theatre, watching the students who did not even sense her stare. The pretty girls with their big titties – she'd always wanted big titties. The guys had funny green hair, messy like they didn't wash or brush it, and they were skinny and laughed so. They were draped in burgundy and green, velvet and crochet, and Alice just wanted to reach out to touch. Their music cases were casually, lovingly brushed against. Another wild peal of laughter rang through the room. Alice propped herself against the entrance and listened shamelessly. She wondered what it would be like, going to the theatre in the evenings and having conversations instead of leaning against the wall by herself.

She felt the weight of his body before she knew he was there. The lanky awkwardness of the evening guard pinned her to the wall.

"Get off." She pushed at him. He dangled the keys above her and snatched them away as she reached out for them.

"You're supposed to be watching the building, not those *moffies*." He rubbed himself against her. His coarse, pale-pink face was touching hers and she was glad she could not see it, nor his small piggy eyes.

"Leave me alone," she said tiredly.

She slipped away from him and grabbed the theatre keys. The barman was standing crossly at the street exit. She nodded towards him and said kindly, "Go."

The students walked past the barman towards the cold outside air, taking their noise and laughter with them. Their movements were marked by a discordant grace: somebody swayed, somebody shook, but they had individual rhythms – they were not in harmony.

She was left alone then.

In her slow and precise way, Alice shut the door between the theatre and the bar, locked it and went down the stairs to the foyer to begin her nightwatch.

Every night she rehearsed her strange dance, not quite knowing or understanding why she had to perform particular movements. The routine was orchestrated by an invisible puppeteer and it was for the guards to perform. Alice had to see that all the locked doors remained locked. Every hour she had to walk up to the Arena and the bar, then to the office block, and then shine her torch at the sliding doors to check for hooligans loitering in the outside amphitheatre. Then she went to see that the basement parking door and backstage access door remained bolted. The lights for the outside area were turned off at one to cut the electricity costs. After each area she had to return to the foyer and shine her torch around for about three minutes. She had to sign the Occurrence Book after each check, stating that each twenty-minute walkabout had been perfectly performed. She was there mainly to deter any potential thieves simply by her presence, so she spent most of her time quietly positioned in the foyer. Here Alice had a view of all the entrances and exits; she could not understand all the fuss about checking to see that locked doors stayed locked, because no one could get into the building without her seeing them if she just stayed put. But she preferred walking about because she could not bear the idea of waiting for an intruder. And because it was so terribly dull to sit and wait. The chairs were not very comfortable either. So she listened to the radio and this was where she usually, but not always, heard the mysterious train and the voice of Luke Loyola.

She liked the thought of him awake with her at three in the morning. She would imagine him, a stocky little bundle, walking home in the dark. He would be hunched into his jacket with his hands in his pockets, thinking difficult thoughts. His path home was slow and careful but not because he feared crime – that would not bother him. Rather, he would be looking at the sea and pondering its mysteries.

There were similarities between them, she liked to think. She considered herself a creature of the night: her nightlife did not disguise the soft, calm voice of the night with noise, but endured its unbearable gentleness. She saw herself as a guardian of the night, keeping watch while everyone else slept. She thought that this was what priests did in some ways. Like a shepherd, the good shepherd who watched her flock, she kept watch over this sterile stone building.

Alice had tried to find out as much as she could about the Kumo Kirk, the community that Luke Loyola's father ran. But they were a quiet group and did not canvass for converts. A visit to the Kirk happened exclusively by invitation. And Alice did not feel a likely candidate for an invitation. She had only completed her schooling until standard eight and had worked at a butchery, a bakery and a petrol station before joining Doubleday Security Services. Here she had climbed the security ladder as she moved from car guard to day building watch to night building watch. She was studying the manual so that she could be promoted to people watch. (She was already training but they thought her a bit shy; she didn't see what shy had to do with anything since all she had to do was watch.)

Still, the building was too quiet. This stillness ached and Alice longed for movement. Not just the shadows moving at the corners of her eyes but the creaks of real footsteps, known footsteps, a newspaper rustling, the taste of shared air. She wanted the room around her to be filled with another living presence. She did not care too much for chatter. She just wanted the burden of space to be shared. The building was cold. The stern brick walls and large sheets of frosty glass embraced her with their cold care. She felt as though she was alone in the pit of a great fish's belly, like Jonah or Pinocchio.

But quite unlike the belly of a great fish, the theatre walls were made of brick and glass. And after Alice turned out the outside lights, the foyer was lit up like a display case. For the man in the shadows outside, Alice was framed as if in a glass cage. It was not that he was very interested in watching her – there was not much of particular interest in a security guard in a sleeping theatre. But Bradley was cold and tired and that little corner of the amphitheatre sheltered him nicely from the wind. He looked down into the foyer; Alice was staring blankly ahead, her legs curled up in the plastic chair. Then she sighed and raised herself and began moving to each locked door once again. She came towards him as she walked up the stairs to the amphitheatre and shone her torch lazily. The beam of light fell, uninspired, onto the ground and did not sweep the corners.

Alice walked away, yawning and stretching her back, and continued the rest of her dance. She returned to the foyer and positioned herself in the chair again and fixed her eyes directly ahead. It amused him to see her lacklustre steps, as though she only walked because someone prodded her from behind. He regarded her sitting in the foyer, watching dully, and thought that there was not much difference between guards and prisoners. Then he turned away and tried to sleep.

Alice was dreaming of Luke Loyola. Her morose stare veiled the less sedate scenes inside her. She stashed a set of stories in her mind and played them back like soap operas to entertain her while she watched the building. That night she was watching "The Great Rescue", where she saves him from an attack, he saves her from a life of drudgery and they talk about complicated things all through the night. Sometimes he was walking home in the dark, sometimes in an exotic garden, but the end was always the same – they talked and talked. That was the sweet climax. She could picture the detail of the surroundings, of their clothes, but never their faces. She had not seen his and she could only ever remember a vague outline of her own. She once pictured a rare flash of his straight strong nose and curved lip, but the details were obscured by his jacket collar. She knew the details of their conversation, the moments when she gently outwitted him and he would shake his head in disbelief and admiration.

It was not easy to sleep on the concrete bench outside. Bradley would have preferred even the orange chair in which Alice shifted uncomfortably. His legs were too long and he had to keep them bent, which gave him a knee cramp. He sat up in frustration and his eye caught the guard, still sitting with both legs crossed and eyes shut. He thought he saw an idiot's smile linger about her lips and then disappear. He checked his watch – it was two o'clock – and wondered if she would check the amphitheatre again.

When he next saw her, she was walking up the stairs, even more listlessly than before. This time she didn't bother shining the torch at all. She seemed to be sleepwalking, oblivious to what she was doing. He ignored her for a while and then found her taking huge gulping sips from a hip flask. Bradley smiled. Watching Alice was not riveting, but he was enjoying her careless approach to her work. He had given up on trying to fall asleep. He wished that she were sexy. He would enjoy watching her then. Then he could imagine her unbuttoning that stiff shirt.

Alice had been telling Luke what she thought about God and the sea. He was listening carefully, his head cocked to the side. Then the smudge that was his face turned quickly away. Someone else had entered the fantasy. This face was defined and its sharpness amplified by the slanting eyes and strong cheekbones. Alice was furious that Jessica should dare. She was about to scream at her, get out of my dream, when Jessica said, "Well, we aren't paying you to sit around thinking dirty thoughts," and smiled triumphantly. Alice woke up startled. That was the first time that she had fallen asleep on duty. Her body temperature had dropped while she slept and she was freezing. She found her hip flask in her bag and took a few slugs of the whisky inside. She was tired and cross with herself for falling asleep, and furious with Jessica for trespassing. Her 01h40 check was half an hour late; she would have to lie when she signed the walkabout in the occurrence book. She moved slowly through the building, not bothering to check anything, just walking the path, an abandoned marionette struggling to move by itself. She returned to the foyer and signed for 01h40 instead of 02h30 and, after briefly hesitating, decided to sign for the 02h40 check as well, taking care to use a different pen. She went back to the foyer, turned her little radio on and jigged about to keep herself warm. The community station was playing windy spiritual music. It made Alice colder. Outside the wind was screaming in a way that unsettled her. When the wind touched the building it emitted a sharp long screech. The glass seemed unsteady against such force.

The cold came through the great glass walls and fingered her gently. The floor was made of stone slabs and the building was cruel in winter. Alice was fed up with the uniform that wasn't warm enough and the stupid plastic chairs that nobody could comfortably spend a night in. But then she supposed that was the aim – to make the guards as uncomfortable as possible. Only the senior staff were allowed to be comfortable. They had a lounge with a mini-bar and television. She knew that it would not be quite as chilly in there. Alice looked longingly at the staff lounge. She was not allowed to go into the lounge, but as the guard on duty, she had a key and thought she could just take a look. See maybe if they had some sherry and remind herself just how fucked up it all was that she had to stay in the dim foyer with a plastic chair and frozen nipples.

It was a nice room, she saw as she entered – tentatively, as though she feared there might be someone inside. There were big, soft couches which promised to warm cold and tired little girls: come to me my pretty and I will eat you up. Seduced by the promise of comfort, Alice made her way to a couch, thinking, take me, take me, aware that she should turn back but helpless. Her tumble into the iniquity of a great swallowing couch was abruptly halted when she noticed a cabinet that bore the name of Jessica Warlock. She opened the cabinet and found an old yellow bag. Alice took the bag, her heart beating excitedly. As a guard she always knew that she could enter all locked doors and discover the secrets held inside, but she had never done this before. She opened the bag. Inside there was a pair of running shoes and some folded clothes. So much for penetrating secrets, she thought. Musty old clothes and dirty tackies. Oh yes, Jessica Warlock, I've got you now. They were gym clothes and they were crumpled and yellowed as though they had been in the cabinet for many months. Alice raised the sweat towel to her nose: it smelt only of the yellow bag. She unfolded the clothes to look at the labels. Jessica Warlock probably never bought her clothes at the Fashion Bin. She picked up a pair of grey cotton panties and inhaled deeply. Still the same musty smell of the bag, vaguely tempered with something else. She held them to her face, and then, on impulse, spat into the crotch. She couldn't believe that she had dared. She stared at the spit and smeared it into the panties. The uninspired sporty grey was just a shade darker. Putting the bag away, she left the lounge feeling odd.

Again, she looked into the still, stony stare of the brick and glass. Her ears were ringing very loudly. She stepped on something soft. It shrieked and she saw the glinting eyes of a cat. She kicked the cat and it flew through the air, screaming shrilly. The deep rumbling train accompanied the scream. Three o'clock. She turned on her little radio.

". . . inspiration by Luke Loyola."

The voice was thin and without accent.

"Brethren, let us love one another. Love is the source of true life. Love moves through the wind, is the current that allows the water to flow, is the fire within the flame and in the earth which sustains us."

They were similar, Alice and Luke. Both were driven by their passions in the small hours of the morning. As Luke spread his message of love, Alice was immersed in the pettiness of her dislike. The smallness of her passion stunned her as she listened. Luke's words came through the little radio, and she looked for the cat so that she could love it and take away her horror of herself. Then the reality of its presence struck her: how did the cat get in? Afraid, she patted her baton and walked slowly through the foyer. At the entrance to the offices, glass lay shattered on the polished stone floor.

Doubleday Security Services did not require their security guards to catch criminals – they just needed them to watch out for them. Between the watching and the evidence there was an unmapped distance. Alice had never been faced with this before and she was not quite sure what to do. Her hands fumbled at her waist, trying to release the baton there. She could not remember the instructions in the manual. She moved slowly towards her bag, baton raised. She pulled the manual from her bag and found it under section 6.2. "In the event of a break-in," she read, relieved. "6.2.1. Ensure you keep a steady eye open." Not easy, Alice thought, when you have to read the manual at the same time. "6.2.2. Ensure you have a means of inflicting harm." She was pleased she had that much. "6.2.3. Have eyes behind your back at all times." Not too useful, that one. The final point, 6.2.4, stated: "Proceed to the reception area, raise the phone handset, dial 0 and call Bill Doubleday on his cellphone immediately." Beneath this, in imperative capitals it shouted: "DO NOT, DO NOT AT ANY POINT ATTEMPT TO PURSUE THE OFFENDER(S) WITHOUT BACK-UP!"

Bill Doubleday was a grumpy bear when woken up at three in the morning, and she did not know how she could explain what had happened. He slept with his hand on his gun, his pretty wife had complained, and jumped up ready for blood when he received a midnight call. Alice would rather wait until morning with a possible intruder than call beefy Bill with his bloodlust. She skimmed through the manual and found, under 7.1, "In the event of an accidental confrontation with offender(s)." Point 7.1.1 read: "Don't look the offender(s) in the eye. This will aggravate him/her."

The shards of glass at the office door were trampled and crushed. Alice hoped this meant that the offender(s) had left the building. She went towards the offices and nervously peeped her head around the door. There was no one there. The accountants' desks were lined up neatly but in their usual papery mess; the theatre's financial records lay in heaps of paper on the floor, but that was their filing system and not a result of the break-in. The lock on the safe was damaged but not broken. Alice left the office and went to check the entrances.

The staff entrance was wide open. There were no cars or people outside, just the dark outline of the trees and swishing leaves. The cold air stung her cheeks and she retreated. She forced herself to do a walkabout, with a cautious stiffness. As she danced the dance the familiarity of the movements brought her some relief. This time they were over-precise, exaggerated so that her sense of the normal could return. The ritualised steps brought their own magic. The other doors were all locked, the shadows were where they belonged, neither smaller nor bigger than usual, and everything was as it should be. She went to the amphitheatre and that was where she found him.

Alice stood before the glass doors of the amphitheatre and felt the gnawing of inadequacy. She would have preferred to battle real villains, with gold-capped teeth and guns, than her own carelessness. She stood before the doors and the blackness beyond and was faced with an image of herself entrapped within the glass. Alice stared back at Alice, with the reflection of the light fittings obscuring her eyes. She thought of the amphitheatre in the summer, when it was filled with happy children who delighted over and over again in the same old stories, and it all seemed so bleak, so desolate.

Where would she go now, what would she do? It wasn't fair, she thought angrily. It wasn't fair that she was a failed security guard, it wasn't her fault. She felt a victim of a far greater crime, greater than this, greater than apartheid, the slow stupid beast; it was as great as fate itself. There, she thought, there, I lay the sodding bundle at your door, God, you sort it out.

She thumped her hand against the door to punctuate her thoughts, and saw the shadow in the corner stir. It moved its head like a giant slug feeling its way. She regarded it, her incurious face lit with rare interest.

Bradley did not sense her as she unlocked the door. It was only when she stood above him that he waded through the confusion and recognised the guard he had watched earlier. She had broken out of her gilded cage and looked down on him with mad eyes. He put his hands up behind his head and said, "Hello girl, come share a little, where's that drink?"

She silently examined him, trailing her eyes over his body, his face and dirty brown clothes.

"You must be so cold," she said.

He thought that maybe he was right, she looked a bit like an idiot. It was unnerving to have her stare and stare. He did not like this strange sympathy.

"Come and get some," she said and walked away. She waited for him at the door and he followed. He wanted a smoke and the thought of the whisky dispelled his wariness. When he was inside, she locked the door and said, "Come into the foyer."

Alice kept a few steps ahead of him and when they reached the foyer she nodded at the plastic chair. "Sit."

She gave him the hip flask and said, "There's more, just wait here."

She went to the door that she had disappeared through earlier and took her baton and jammed it against the lock until the padlock broke. She smiled and said that she had locked the key inside. When she came out, she had rope and a bottle of brandy. He was savouring his cigarette when he felt her behind him.

"Hey man! What are you doing?" he shouted as he felt the rope cutting through his jacket into his abdomen.

"Apprehending criminals," she said sweetly. She held out the brandy and sloshed it over his jacket.

"What? Are you befok? Watch it! This is my work jacket."

"Oops," she smiled, "must have missed your mouth. There, have some more." She held the bottle to his mouth and poured it down his throat. Bradley spluttered. Then she took a swig and said, "I am so happy to have found you, I could kiss you." She put her drink-flavoured mouth to his and kissed him, long and hard, like a movie hero. The brandy burned in his chest and he struggled to breathe as she pushed her tongue into his mouth.

"Mmmmmm," she said, "tastes like brandy."

"So," she clapped her hands together, "I'm Alice, what's your name? What do you do? Where are you from? Why were you outside my building? We have another two hours together so we can talk."

Each question was asked with the cadence of a child pondering great mysteries. He was enraged. "You let me go right now, this is illegal."

She loved the way his face revealed his frustration. The skin around his eyes wrinkled just the way she liked it: she wanted to trace the lines with her fingers.

"I think what *you've* done is illegal, but then I don't know that much about the law. What I do know is retribution and justice. God gives you what you deserve. Or maybe not. I don't know, what do you think?"

96

Bradley did not quite feel that he could answer this. It seemed insane to discuss God while tied up and drenched in brandy.

He was silent for a while and then she leaned forward. "Why don't you answer me?"

He shrugged his shoulders. "Please just let me go. I will leave now, really. I missed the last train and just needed to get out of that wind. I'm sorry I slept outside your building, truly, just let me go home."

"You missed your train," she leaned forward. "Do you mean the three o'clock train that goes by every morning?"

He did not mean that at all, no passenger train went by at three in the morning, but there was something about the way she leaned towards him that made him tell the lie.

"Yes, the three in the morning train, that's the one I usually take."

"Does it go all the way to Simon's Town ?"

He wasn't sure what answer she wanted, so he tentatively ventured: "Yes?"

She threw her fists in the air and echoed his "Yes!", but with a glee he couldn't possibly summon.

"So this train gets to Fish Hoek at 03h37, doesn't it? Does anyone get on the train in Fish Hoek at 03h37?"

He could tell that she desperately wanted someone to get on this train.

"There are some people who get on at Fish Hoek, ja. A woman, a man . . ."

"What does the man look like? Do they get on together?" She was excited now.

"No, they're not together. It's very difficult to tell what he looks like because he is always bundled up in his jacket," he lied desperately.

"I knew it, I knew it!"

She moved away from him and sat down quietly. He was relieved by the silence for a while, and then she said, "Please talk to me, I would really like it if you talked to me."

He remembered those FBI agents on TV who, when kidnapped by maniacs, used psychological tricks to get themselves free.

"Well, if we're going to chat then you must give me another smoke, because that always makes me feel more sociable, maybe some more of that brandy, and you need to take this rope off me, because how can we *skinder* if I'm all tied up?" He shrugged his shoulders in what felt like a charming way.

She shook her head. "My job comes first."

He asked her to reach into his pocket for his pills; he needed to take them for his blood pressure, he said. She found the yellow plastic packet that the clinics used to dispense drugs and was reminded of her grandfather. The smell of the man, the way he twisted the yellow bag in his hands, was marked with the same tired care. She almost felt sorry for him then; she would have hated for this to happen to her grandfather. His eyes were so brown that the colour spilt out onto the white bits. His heavy jacket and trousers were stained from years of public transport, from the hard benches of Coloured Affairs, free clinics and other Government waiting rooms.

Alice smiled at him in a way that seemed so lonely, so lost, and said, "Please tell me about Luke Loyola on the train."

Bradley started telling stories that he didn't know. He told her how the man always sat in the same seat and stared out of the window and looked at the sea. He never spoke, he dealt with the drunks with great dignity and he was light of step, with the grace of a dancer.

"He's not a *moffie*," she said indignantly.

With Alice dropping clues, Bradley was able to tell her about how Luke Loyola comforted a sobbing woman on the train, how he spoke to the poor and broken-hearted and healed the imaginary people on what must have been a goods train that passed by the theatre at three every morning.

When Beefy Bill Doubleday arrived at five o'clock with the day guard, he found an oddly satisfied Alice in the foyer with a booze-stained man tied to a plastic orange chair.

The tedium of work sustained Mr Kapp. Sorting papers into piles neatly bound by paper clips and arranging them into files allowed him several hours of silence. There were pages and pages of numbers written in his own neat handwriting on A4 sheets torn from a note book. He understood numbers better than words. All day he filled his head with numbers, which obliterated words from his head and made him distrust them. This made him uncertain about whether he could communicate through the vague sums and equations of letters and words. They simply weren't viable, not the way numbers were, he thought. He spoke slowly and cautiously, with a tendency to repeat himself. When he uttered a sentence, the blankness he perceived on his audience's faces made him panic that he wasn't understood, that people could not hear him. He feared that this was extended to his presence, that if he wasn't heard, he wasn't seen either. That the only way he was realised was by his pages of figures, which functioned as the great cogs in the machine of the theatre's dwindling finances. Before he could be snuffed out by untrustworthy words and lazy ears, he doubled his efforts by echoing everything that he uttered.

"Good morning, good day," he boomed from his big lungs and tall, thick body. He did not stop to see if anyone had heard him before going through to the director's office.

Ken Crane, on the other hand, had a short circuit between brain and speech. He thought fast and his mouth could not keep up with the speed of his mind. What emerged from his mouth were very quick sentences which often missed a word or two as they tripped out. Jessica Warlock's duties included interpreting the often garbled speech of Mr Kapp and Mr Crane. Indeed, more often than not, she spoke for them.

Alice had never really seen the office from this perspective. For the first time she noticed details – the paintings on the wall, the plants on the windowsill and the books on the shelves. Rows of books lined the walls, and she wondered if Ken Crane had really read any of them.

She was sitting on a soft leathery couch that she had never been allowed to sit on before. A tray of coffee and biscuits was placed next to her. She wished she was standing. Mr Crane was standing above her, just near enough for her to feel his presence. Bill from Double-day was on the other side, his hairy hands rubbing his bald head. But Mr Crane and beefy Bill were dwarfed by Jessica, taking notes in the corner. Alice helped herself to a biscuit, feeling her stomach twist as she bit into it.

"Alice, padlock broken?" Ken Crane's small face hovered above hers, as though he could read the answer there more quickly than hearing her speak it.

"Excuse me sir?" Alice said through a mouth filled with biscuit she wished she hadn't taken.

"Mr Crane is enquiring how the padlock to the staff room was broken," Jessica said, also looking at her intently. There were lines beneath Jessica's eyes and Alice remembered her drunken departure from the bar.

Alice launched into her prepared explanation: "The three damaged doors were broken into in a period of twenty minutes. This must have occurred just after I began the building check at 02h40. I assume that while I was upstairs, he broke into the staff lounge. When I returned to the foyer, I found the door open. I went inside but saw no one. I then went to check the staff entrance, the only door I hadn't yet checked. I found it open and damaged. I went outside to make sure that no one was lurking there. When I returned to the foyer, I found that the offices had been broken into. I found him in there, trying to break into the safe." It seemed too easy, too flawless.

Mr Kapp was nodding his head. "Why didn't you call for help, my girl, why didn't you get your boss on the scene of the crime? Dangerous, dangerous, a little thing like you."

This was the weak point. She had disobeyed orders by not calling Bill.

"I think that Mr Kapp has a good point there," said Jessica, "but more importantly, had you called for help, as you were supposed to, the minute you saw the damage to the staff lounge, we might have avoided the damage to the offices. It's going to cost us a fortune to have the damaged doors replaced, especially the office glass doors and safe."

Alice regarded Jessica with her practised look of dumb insolence.

"I'm sorry, I just followed my instincts," she said. Let Jessica think her slow and dull, incapable of thought.

Alice caught a hint of her perfume. But for Alice, the smell of musty once-worn panties would forever linger beneath the expensive scent. She looked Jessica firmly in the eye. She was certain that Jessica did not remember her – why should she?

Jessica had been staring at her unashamedly, and now shuffled the papers in front of her.

"Your criminal," she said, "Bradley Thomas, claims that he did not break into the building at all. He says that he simply missed the last train home and fell asleep outside the building."

Alice was ready for this. "Well, do you expect him to simply confess? He was drunk, you can see that he is a dirty thief. I was just doing my job."

"Jessica, he was reeking of alcohol," Bill said wearily.

"Well, his version is that Alice poured the drink down his throat."

At this, all three men burst into laughter. "Yes, that's what I sometimes tell my wife," Ken Crane said and they all laughed again. This time Alice joined in and the sound echoed around the room. Only Jessica did not laugh.

"We will take care of things from here on. Thank you, Alice, for a superb performance. A good job, girl, we're pleased to have you on our team, very pleased. You will reward her, Bill, make sure she gets what she deserves."

Jessica was silent as she watched Alice leave the office, grabbing another biscuit as she left. Alice walked out to the foyer almost singing aloud. She went to the security office to write her report and found Bradley in an orange chair. There was a woman with him, her eyes thick and tired.

"I don't know, Bradley, I don't know what to think," she was saying as Alice entered the room. She fell silent as Bill and Alice walked in. Both Bradley and his wife knew only too well how to be silent.

There was a moment where Alice felt deeply sorry that Bradley had been so ill-treated by fate. She leaned to him and said, "God will give you what you deserve, just wait and see, it will be okay."

She caught a glimpse of the Occurrence Book on the table. She remembered that she had signed in the 02h40 check, saying that everything was in order. She felt the hair on her arms stand on end. But then she let it go. That was easy to get around. Besides, they would not notice anything that they did not want to.

She left the room then and moved along the now bright staircase. The daylight was streaming into the building and the cold stoniness disappeared. There were people moving about, performing their own sequences, and the building did not watch. There were too many of them now. The door of the staff lounge was open and it had lost all air of sacred space. She did not care so much about her bad behaviour now. She thought of her self-proclaimed status as guardian of the night and laughed because it all seemed silly. At the doors to the amphitheatre, she paused and went outside. On the concrete bench where she had found Bradley, she saw a yellow plastic bag with some pills inside. She was right, they did not notice anything they did not want to. Alice picked up the bag and folded it into a tiny square. Then she pushed it deep into her pocket and went home to sleep. They had given her the night off and she planned to be at the train station in Fish Hoek at 03h37. She needed her rest.

The Woodcutter's Daughter

There in the iron forest, they played this game.

Julia was a pleasant child, the seventh daughter of a woodcutter. The woodcutter lived in the forest, in a house fashioned from a sprawling oak tree. But he did not simply chop wood: he was a skilled craftsman and could bewitch any old dry piece of wood into something beautiful. He took a great pride in his work and an even greater pride in his daughters. His girls were happy – they worked hard and wanted for nothing. They had a lake in their front garden and a river at the back.

Julia was, for all her pleasantness, a dark child. Her eyes were wider and blacker than the others'. She alone roamed further than the tree house.

One day, as she rambled after all her chores were done, she found a gate hidden beneath a blanket of leaves. The gate was carved of wood and showed the most exquisite craftsmanship. Because Julia was an honest carpenter's daughter, she exclaimed at the beauty of the design.

"Oh," she whispered as she traced the intricate pattern etched into the wood. She pushed and pulled at the gate but she could not open it. She frowned and skipped away, meaning to tell her sisters. But that evening, as they supped in the tree house, she felt fierce possessiveness and could not say a word.

As she lay in her white wooden bed, after saying her prayers, she imagined all sorts of possibilities.

Imagine, she whispered to herself, that whoever passed through the gate would not ever die.

Imagine, there is a faerie kingdom on the other side.

Imagine that a princess is suffering an enchantment and is enduring until I rescue her.

Imagine that an old woman, my true mother the queen, waits in exile behind one hundred golden doors.

Julia thought so much that she slept very little. The next day she was cross and tired. She was mean to her sisters, who were of a milder temperament than she with her fiery mind: she spoke back snappily and even pinched poor Amber, making her cry. She ran off as soon as she'd angered them and they refused to bear her company. She ran back to her gate.

Again, she fingered its beauty. Again she pushed and pulled but without success. She tried to climb over, she tried to cut through the trees, to climb around (for she was a clever child and not likely to sit still and cry). She even tried to dig a tunnel underneath, but there were too many rocks blocking the way.

Exhausted, she conceded defeat and kicked at the gate in rage. But the gate was built of strange wood and would not relent.

That night she refused supper; her face was red and fevered and she would not speak. Once everyone was asleep, she slipped out of her white wooden bed and ran to the gate.

The moonlight coloured the gate white. Julia knew of the dangers of the forest and was afraid. She sat down on the rocks near the gate because she didn't know what else to do. She could not leave because she would be miserable if she did. She shivered in the cold wind and curled up below the gate. Julia felt so alone beside that gate. She longed for the sound of her sisters' laughter, the sighs of their breathing in the beds next to hers. She fell asleep for a while, but she was a restless sleeper and kept rolling onto rocks and stones that dug into her body.

She cried out in annoyance as stones burrowed into her back. She sat up and cleared them away, throwing first one, then another, and then a furious hail of stones at the gate.

It was only after she had thrown it that she remembered the smooth metal hurled from her fingers: the three large clover leaves at the end; the long, thick spine; the fine protrusions that held the only code that would be read by the waiting lock. At last, the key: the missing part to match the hidden grooves.

Triumphantly, she marched to the gate, her whole body trembling with excitement. She pushed the key into the lock and it turned slowly and with great difficulty. When she finally pushed the gate open, a curious heat started deep in her belly; the sound of her beating heart echoed inside her head. She stepped through and onto the other side.

It was twilight on the other side of the gate. The shadows of the autumn trees were long fingers waving on the ground. She walked bravely, but a voice inside her told her to stay in the shadows of the trees, only walk in the shadows: untold dangers lay in the light. It was then that she noticed the moss. The path beneath her feet was covered by it. Moss grew on the trees and covered every corner with its velvet comfort.

Julia heard voices. She could not hear what they were saying. Then she saw the shape of two lovers in the garden. They walked closely, each one intoxicating the other, the way lovers do. They were an enchanted couple; they did not keep inside the shadows. A light shone in the distance – it seemed that they were walking towards it. Julia slunk further into the shadows, afraid to break the aloneness of their twilight stroll. As they came towards her, the lady lover tilted her head and said, "We have walked this garden for three thousand nights now. Why is it that tonight I feel so strange?"

Julia saw her face and was surprised: it was the face of her own sister Amber, yet it was different. She saw the same eyes, the same round childlike cheeks, but it was not her sister. The lady lover had a forlornness in her face that Amber would never have. Julia longed for her sister then, so she turned around and ran back to the gate. When she returned to the tree house, she slept deeply next to Amber all through the night and woke up the next morning uncertain if she had dreamed it all. She did her chores the next day with an unusual vigour, impatient for the night to fall. At last the evening came and she could return to the gate. She slipped her hand into her pocket and felt for the key deep in its fold.

The garden gave off a scent of beauty that made her feel drunk. She wandered about the garden, which seemed to have no boundaries. She wandered for hours, keeping no track of the time. The twilight did not fade into night. There were strange birds singing beautiful, lonely songs. Julia came across the lovers walking in the garden again. As they passed the rose bush behind which she hid, the lady lover's hand fluttered to her chest and she said, "Oh, there it is again. I cannot say what it is that possesses me but suddenly I am filled with sadness, with a sense of loss, an ache for someone very dear, yet I do not know —"

The man was upset and said, "We have to leave the garden now. You know that no sadness nor sorrow is allowed here."

Slowly they made their way down the path. Julia longed to call after them and see where the path went, why it was only for them that the distant light shone. But then she thought she heard the voice of her sister and, keeping in the shadows of the trees, she ran back to the other side of the gate.

Amber was awake in her bed: she squeezed her sister's arm as she climbed in beside her. She begged, she implored, but Julia would not tell of her secret garden of moss.

The third night, Julia once again crept out of her bed. But when she left the room, Amber threw back the covers and followed her. Julia yet again went through the white gate, but this time, as the gate fell back, Amber's little foot caught it just in time and she followed Julia through.

Julia wandered through the twilight forest, safely keeping in the shadows of the trees. Again she stroked the moss as she walked, feeling the texture beneath her fingers. Again she saw the lovers walk through the garden and again, as they drew near to where she hid behind a rose bush, the lady lover became agitated, saying that she could feel someone else there. The man was cross. He told her that there was no one else; that no one in the world knew of their secret garden. The lady lover seemed sad; her eyes told of a misfortune that Julia could not understand but longed to console. Julia realised then that the lady lover was trapped in an enchantment. Just as she was about to call to her, she heard a scream.

Julia turned, as did the lovers, to see Amber lying inert in a patch of moonlight. The man grabbed the lady lover's arm and led her towards that light, moving speedily. Julia was torn between chasing after them and going to Amber. She moved towards Amber and saw that she had not kept in the shadows of the trees. Now she had to dare: in order to reach Amber, she had to step into the light. The ground felt hot. As she moved closer to Amber, there was a blazing heat that shot up through her legs until eventually she felt she was on fire – and then nothing.

She awoke to find herself on a bed of moss, with veils of leaves and vines twisting themselves into a shelter. She awoke to find the finely stitched blanket of moss covering her, with Amber nowhere in sight. She awoke to see a pair of magnificently arched eyebrows above her.

"I kissed you so that you would awake, and now you must be my wife." A dark man knelt beside her.

"But I am not an enchanted princess," she objected. "I would have risen of my own accord."

"That does not matter."

She blushed, because she felt a bit impolite. Maybe he was just trying to be nice.

"I think I might have seen one, an enchanted princess, back there," she added helpfully. "If you set out now, you might just find her."

"She has already been claimed," her prince replied. "This is an enchanted garden and you must abide by the rules of this world. And here, should any man rouse a woman with a kiss, she is his."

Julia did not care much for his words, but she conceded that this was his world and she was a guest and her father had raised her to have perfect manners. She had no intention of being his wife and hoped that he would lead her to Amber, and perhaps some food. So she draped herself in the moss blanket and walked with him, and in the manner of enchanted worlds found herself transformed: with each step they took, she was more and more drawn to him. With each step she forgot more about Amber. First she forgot her name – she knew she had to find her sister, but could not remember what she was called. Then she forgot that it was her sister; then she forgot that she had to find someone. Then she only remembered that there was something she was trying to remember. Then she forgot even that.

The prince took her to his house, which was made of carved wood and filled with furniture crafted with the most beautiful patterns. Julia expressed delight as she ran her fingers over the designs. "Whose is the skill behind such beauty?" she asked breathlessly, for it exceeded even her father's talent.

"It is your husband's," he smiled. "The carvings on the wood tell a story that I will tell you in good time."

They feasted on a wedding supper of succulent summer fruits: nectarines, peaches, plums and mangoes. There were melons (green, pink and orange), litchis, grapes and pineapples – all of which were perfectly ripened and unblemished. They drank a warm and spicy wine that burned in the pit of Julia's stomach. He robed her in a beautiful gown that was made of the same fabric as the moonlight. They sat on a veranda overlooking the twilight garden: the air was heavy with the scent of a thousand flowers. She was happy and did not remember her sisters.

Julia bathed in rose petals and milk as she prepared herself for her wedding night. The fragrance of petals clung to her as she climbed the candle-lit staircase to the bridal chamber. This time she was wearing a dress made of starlight that trailed up the stairs behind her. She climbed slowly but purposefully because she was nervous but had a bold heart. She did not stop to pause outside the door of their room. Instead she swept in and saw her lover waiting in a bed hung with red velvet curtains.

Why does he not rise to meet me? she thought.

She reached the bed and still he did not rise. She leaned over him and saw that he did not move at all. She took his hand – it was cold. She climbed on top of him so that she could share her warmth. But the heat did not sear his eyes open. Ice had frozen his blood and it could not be melted.

Julia wept beside him for many days. She did not notice the time go by; she did not feel any hunger. When she ran out of tears and her voice was used up with weeping, she finally heard another soft voice that had sung all the while. She looked around to see where the sound came from, but she could not find it. She searched the house: upended book shelves, tore down heavy curtains; but still the little voice continued to sing its low song. Julia slowly realised that the song was louder when she touched certain things and softer when she didn't. She realised then that she heard the song not through her ears, but through her fingers. She traced the textures beneath her hands. Was it the velvet? The wrought iron twisted into tortured designs?

Of course, she exclaimed when she finally remembered. The wood. It was the wood singing to her. She went to the veranda to find the beginning. She traced her husband's wood carvings with her blistered hands. She listened for a long time. She listened quietly until she had heard the story of the wood as it sang in its soft woody voice. Then Julia prepared herself to set out into the moss garden – she knew what she had to do.

But that was not meant to be. Julia never did save the enchanted maiden, nor did she find her precious Amber. She did not revive her beloved craftsman.

Annette was crying. The game was over. Jessica was torn between consoling Annette and her quest to save the bewitched creatures in her garden. In the end she did neither: she went to a corner of the metal yard and twisted some copper wire into a snake. She played by herself. Annette cried quietly – just big watery eyes spilling with no sound – until the older girls noticed. They took her back into their domestic fantasy and continued making pretend stews, chopping wood and sunning themselves beside a sheet of rippled zinc. They did not know of the hidden gate or of the twilight garden. Only Annette knew Jessica's secret game.

It was too late. Her twilight kingdom had vanished – it had vanished while unresolved. She felt ineffectual: her lady lover remained trapped in an enchantment and would remain unhappy; her charmed husband would forever linger in his icy bed. She was frustrated that she could not even imagine herself into a different space without making it all go wrong. But, she thought as she twisted the copper, what could she do? Her face was morose – her cheeks heavy and her chin determined. Nothing, she told herself. Annette had stopped crying and was laughing with her sisters. The older sisters were absorbed in their game and paid no attention to Jessica sulking in the corner.

Jessica sat by herself in the metal yard and wished that the other girls would call her. But they did not, so she played alone and made herself forget.

Beesting

Oleander rises, drops her skirt, and pads on to catch up, her ungainly gait cast off when she shed her other skin, her other name. She is lean and shorn now, just a bristly soft fur spreads across her head. Eve cuts ahead, winging her way through the prickly spring growth that inches tentatively across the path. Tina, who has become Mala, tails behind, lifting the eager branches and neatly placing them down again. Mala's face is as old as parchment and her eyes green as moss. Oleander does not mind the pricks and barbs of the branches snapping back: her skin is thicker than that. Oleander, who used to Alice, is as benign as a small flower.

Eve – no longer Evie – leads the way back to the Kirk Hall after two silent weeks in the hills. Each walks back smiling a secret clutched to her chest; they should each have received a revelation alone in their roughly built shelters, but sometimes with these things it is difficult to tell. Soon they will be initiated into the secret way of the Kirk. Eve's bare foot tramps down, just missing a thick, segmented worm. She sees it in the groove between her toes – saved – and thinks: intimate.

They descend slowly to the Kirk Hall, a building once home to an embarrassment of husbandless mothers, then an experimental laboratory for mental research, then later a nest for degenerate boys and their depraved instructors. A long history as a state-run reformatory of sorts rests uncomfortably, stirs deep in the salmon-pink walls. The Hall lies just on the other side of the red hill and is some distance from the stone Kirk Temple. The Kumo and Kindali families secured the land stretching from the Hall to the reserve in the heyday of the experimental lab. The more able patients were good fun, some of them trekking to the bottom of the hill to lay the foundations of the stone temple; the Kirk had a rather more disagreeable relationship with the ascetic caretakers of the wayward youths, eternally digging in the backyard next door. It was a relief when the Kirk bought and consecrated the Hall, and so sealed themselves off. There are some naval buildings about ten kilometres away, some corrugated-iron shacks have grown next to the forest and a haunted olive farm lies on the far side; but the Kirk sinks unnoticed into the back of the hill. The gravel road that leads to the Hall is a needle-thin crack veering left at the second tree after the third hairpin bend in the road. A cluster of rocks codes a welcome (open sesame) to the rest of the Kirkers who live scattered along the nose of the peninsula.

The initiates return to an empty Hall. The others are on watch in the hives which lie behind the Beekeeper's Lodge. It is the first of the seven days of the Beesting. The three women drink coconut milk and molasses outside in the wild garden. They are wiry and sun-kissed and rest contentedly in the shade of a eucalyptus tree. The sweet molasses dissolves pleasantly into the thick milk and into their depleted veins; the sun is skipping happily between the leaves swishing above them and the breeze is just mild enough. Their orange feet tap lightly on the dirt floor as they sing the humming song.

Ana has taught them the Beesting songs over the last few months, while they worked on the Kirk lands in preparation for the spring festival. They would sit in the smokehouse, curing the meat and learning the songs and rituals of the Beesting, during which they are to be formally initiated and marked as daughters of the Kirk.

"First the Beekeeper sings out to the Queen Bee to find out if she is ready, and the Queen Bee replies that he should leave her alone. Then the Beekeeper waggles to the opposite side and tries again. And again she tells him to leave, but this time she is a bit less adamant. This happens a few times: each time she a bit coyer, he a bit nearer. The Beekeeper and the Queen Bee dance with each other, slowly getting closer while the swarm gradually descends upon the Beekeeper until he is completely covered. He must move gently: if he jerks in the slightest, they will react. But Papa never jerks. Well almost. The rest of us are spread around, beating the ground as we hum the workers' song, softly at first but this builds and builds until it sounds awesome, like a swarm arriving on the crest of a thunderstorm."

Ana then sang out the high notes of the Queen Bee's final surrender in her bright clear voice, shaking her abdomen as the Queen Bee would.

"It's not just a mating dance, it's a dance of creation on a much grander scale, as it dances the world into being. This is just a metaphor, see, we don't really believe that the bees danced and the world was. Each precise movement is an artistic way of saying sciencey things. Now you try."

Ana switched to the busier hum of the workers' song, her lips pursed earnestly, until all three of the initiates could join in.

Now, beneath the gum tree, they sing the different parts fluidly and their thoughts are free of care. Eve is dappled by the light and she is thinking how good it is to return, that coming back casts a radiance: the leaves are that much greener; the Kirk Hall is benevolent and smiles at her as she sits in its shade. She knows the profile of the mountain and she smugly suspects that it has missed her pottering about the Kirk land. She looks at the wooden table and the dangling branches and thinks: just that, I could look at that forever.

Up there in the hills over these last two weeks, in the dewy early-September mornings, Eve has been preparing. She will offer herself – flesh and soul – as a nun to the Kirk, and has carefully practised the initiation rituals. She sees herself working side by side with Luke Loyola as his little helper, ministering to those in need, maybe even outside the Kirk community.

Excited by this, Eve spent her first day of meditation happily daydreaming. But then she was ashamed of herself, and began to question her motives. Eve was not entirely sure whether she sought to serve or whether her most basic drive had always been to make herself feel safe. If she wanted to make some kind of true offer to the Kirk, then perhaps she was deluding herself with thoughts of the value of her soul – why would they want that? Eve suspected that her body was worth more; it had at least a practical use: hands to till the soil, a womb to bear fruit. She thought perhaps she should try to be good, truly good – isn't that what all gods want? Good sheep biding their time in the meadows. But how is anyone capable of being good – beyond a skin-deep smiley kind of niceness – unless they understand what it is to be evil? This thought nagged at her; she could not stop it from intruding on her meditation. She heard it urge her through the wind that howled around her perch overlooking the sea. But maybe (she had a dizzying flash of insight one day as she stood up too quickly), just maybe God was speaking to her. She didn't know how else he spoke other than to sing to her, since Monday, in a gurgly voice from beneath the sea: come, come see the beauty of my creation, my pretty thing, feast your eyes on this splendour, lay your weary soul on my mossy bed. But that was perhaps too repetitive a refrain for a god – surely he had more to say than just that same jolly ditty, over and over again? Oh, she was just a little bit hungry. There, the voice in the wind that called to her so seductively: just try it, it whispered, curling her hair from her face, c'mon, it's as easy as pie, as a chocolate éclair . . . the wind gently raised her skirt, it felt like a cat brushing against her legs. A warm lamb stew with roast potatoes and fruity baked tart. Eve thought that maybe she needed to understand evil. But what could she do? A black bird landed. There alone in her hut on the hills, in the shadowed evening, Eve tried to embrace evil, quietly, quickly, before it was too late.

Maybe it is because Oleander is wearing a bright yellow skirt, or it could be the smell of the sweet tea. The siren call of the song could have lured it – something has attracted the bee. At first Eve can't see it, just hears the low sound weaving in and out of their own bee voices. For a second she thinks: magic. But there it is – a fuzzy bee rising just in and out of their vision. Mala greets it with a little bow, hands clutched to her breast.

"Hello there, little friend, aren't you meant to be up at the hives with the others? Have you come to bring us a message?"

The bee circles away and dips. It flies up and then sinks towards the steaming cup in Oleander's hand. She shrieks, spilling some of the tea, and jerks her hand back. Mala cautions Oleander to be still as the bee hovers above the tea.

"Pull the cup away," she orders as the bee aims again for the steaming cup of sweetness. "If it scalds or drowns . . . ohh, I don't want to think about what will happen then."

Oleander is waving her left arm about in a crazy dance. "Get it away from me. Just get this thing away!"

Mala, nervously now: "Watch your tongue, Oleander. We don't want to offend."

There is a polite smile in her words: don't mind us, little bee.

"Cut the crap, Mala, and get this thing off me, it's just a bee and I think I'm allergic." Shrilly.

"That little thing is more afraid of you than −" False bravado makes Mala's voice shake. "Where is your faith, Oleander?"

"Oh please, Mala, please. Do something. Just get it away." The bee is buzzing furiously. "It's going to sting −"

The sound of the hand slapping the wooden table is a low echo of Oleander's squeal of pain. Mala's face is stinging red, as if Oleander has smacked her instead, and Oleander looks at the remains of the bee stuck on her hand. A bit of bee is stuck to the table. Eve thinks: wingless.

It is a scary rhyme to her own botched attempt at evil. Eve thinks of the feeble fluttering of bird wings cut by glass, her hands stained by her experiment; she remembers herself split in two, at once a bestial, grunting Eve as she tore her way through the feathery flesh, and also curiously detached as she watched the horror her hands worked. She wanted to cut, to pluck the wings off the bird simply for the sake of it. Just to see. But she failed − the wings half torn, half mangled, the bird alive for too long after she had blindly slashed it with a thick shard of glass − which was in its way a worse kind of evil: the stupid kind, a clumsy and tentative evil. At least a familiar touch, an old hand, strikes with precision; the awkward fumbling of a beginner, the cruelty of a schoolyard bully, is more devastating in its ignorance.

"What have you done?"

"It did sting me!" Oleander holds out her hands in disbelief, in supplication, as she examines the hard red skin, the criss-cross of lines, a roadmap of some unknown place. "Please don't tell."

"Your hands are stained with bee blood. During the Beesting!" There is involuntary revulsion in Mala's voice. She is shifty-eyed; she looks at Oleander's knee, then looks away: Oleander transformed by one frantic slap.

"You both just sat there. Why didn't you do something, why didn't you help me?" she keens.

Eventually: "At least you are not allergic, Oleander." Eve may be ham-fisted with evil, but she finds unkindness easy enough.

"They will make me go back." She stabs a finger at Eve's chest, "Out there." The finger is flung out, wildly pointing to the trees, the sky, the sea. "But they can't because I have wanted this too much. So they just can't."

Oleander's eyes are wet black beads made fierce by her angular skull, her thin shoulders heavy. Eve is as mild as ever. She has come to love Mala, with her shock of white hair framing her dark, wrinkled face and startling eyes, but she is wary of Oleander, who is a bit too irregular. Oleander always emerges just one moment too early or late, sings off-key, says the right thing at the wrong time. She pads around silently, surefooted as a little animal, and as skittish. They came to the Kirk as initiates at different times. Oleander arrived first, three years ago. She has endured a lifetime of waiting, she cannot bear waiting: in her other life – before her metamorphosis – there were one hundred years in a dark empty building, an eternity in a deserted midnight train station.

It has been a year since Mala decided to become the wife of Tebogo Cann, the gentle widower from the line of Elijah Kumo, who keeps chameleons in his backyard. Eve came to the Kirk some months ago on a blazing summer evening when the city was coloured sepia and drizzled soot. She has almost come to believe, as the Kirkers whisper, that she was blown in from the sea, that she came down the hill from nowhere, bearing nothing but the clothes on her back. She prefers the half-shaped idea that she wandered out of a myth, some wild unformed place. She likes it more than the other version: the train ride as the early evening brought little reprieve from the heat, the walk up the hill where the ground burned to the touch as the nearby mountains blazed. There is less guilt, less weight. She wants to believe that she has shed those things, that the distance travelled the evening she arrived erased that old story, that the time ticked on since has cleared the wreckage of that strange hot-cold night. When two angels with blazing swords barred the gate to a twilight garden. It was a quiet disaster: a sip of coffee, a hand wiping a mouth with a folded white serviette – and then it was over.

The others have returned. Only Eve is composed, although both Mala and Oleander make an effort to hide their disturbance. Ana sings out to the initiates, welcomes them with a kiss as Oleander wipes her puffy hand down the side of her yellow skirt. Ana loves them all, but especially Eve. She chatters away with her bright voice. While they were away, the Brethren – that's the Kirk Authority, made up of eleven elders from the worldwide Kirk – came and are staying down at the Loyola house, the Cape Dutch homestead a bit further down towards the town. There was something going on, Ana wasn't quite sure; Papa wouldn't tell her and Luke, well he was as dour as ever.

How much Eve loves this place. She would do anything for Ana. They are a pretty picture: the women sitting in the shade of the tree, framed by the wooden bench and the branches dancing just above their heads. Oleander's shoulders turn slightly away, immersed in a sullen silence; Eve snips her from the picture.

Later, alone with Ana, Eve finds out. Eben's hands are unsteady, they have lost the firm grasp that characterised his Beekeeper's dance in previous years. The Beekeeper's grace and steadiness in the slow precise dance had for years been a consolidation of his strength as leader. But the previous year, he had faltered in the small fixed steps that beat out a sacred pattern. It's his hands, he cannot keep them from shaking. Even his stillest moments are unnerved by the tremor in his hands. This year, there was talk of Luke taking over as Beekeeper instead of Smoker and Handler, but the Kirkers weren't enthusiastic – Luke was too uneven in his movements, too jagged in shape – and dancing the Beekeeper's dance was an intricate business. Getting it wrong can be dangerous to the Beekeeper, and one missed step spells trouble. But mostly, there is the sense of something being wrong. That the reason Eben's hands shake is because something is wrong. There is talk of a God who is too silent: no signs, no visions. No word from above. People are whispering too much.

"I hate it when they whisper like that," Ana says. "Papa's getting a bit old, but there is nothing wrong with him. Luke is pretty much running everything these days, I don't know where we'd be without him."

But that was not all. When the Brethren arrived, they had commenced the council and barely performed the opening rites. Ana had been there when they came, hovering in the passage with honey and nutmeg to bless and welcome them, but they did not linger.

"Papa was even wearing his Ndebele-patterned robe, which you know means that he wants to celebrate, and they just went off to the study and talked. No fermented apple for me."

Ana is gloomy when she says, "I am just a little bit nervous."

On the fourth day of the Beesting, Eve is standing beneath the picture of Jezebel at the edge of the cliff when Luke walks into the white Kirk Temple. She looks at him and thinks about winglessness, and suddenly knows two things for certain: moss creeping on a wet black stone; moss against the rough bark of a shaded trunk.

"You can say no," Luke begins. "But it would be better if you didn't. Papa has a very exciting plan for you. You have been blessed." Luke will not look at her. "Once you put your reservations aside, you will soon see how very lucky you are."

"Yes," Eve says, that is all she can give. Yes, but it is yes to Luke alone, anything for Luke.

"Think of it as God's call. Think of it as – as the Kirk's salvation in your hands. As doing your little bit."

There are no words for this, no daisies whose plucked petals can give her a different answer, no divining cards that can be switched so that the outcome could be different. She does not know what to do with this; where is she supposed to put it? It can only be unrequited – he is a monk of the Kirk. She just does not know what she can do other than avoid it, agree to the mysterious request, and maybe seal it away through the tightly structured Kirk rituals. Then she may regard it from a distance, as though someone else's tapestry or sonnet, with all its messiness woven in and restrained. Just an outline roughly sketched, presenting itself in a reassuring single dimension. Quietened, because this is too noisy; everything inside Eve is restless.

On the fifth day of the Beesting the marking ceremony is held, with a huge roaring fire under an evening sky. Female initiates are branded as Kirkers; girls may, if they are considered ready by the Kirk Elders, cross the divide into womanhood. This year Ana is to be marked as a woman. She and Eve will receive twin brands – broad burns across their bellies – their sisterhood and enduring love so etched into the body. Bound by a glowing hot poker and a long, angry-red sear.

On the sixth day of the Beesting, Eve is called to a meeting of the Brethren in the stone Temple. The meeting is just about to begin and Oleander brings in a tray of blessed wine, those claw-like hands stiffly holding the rim. She places the tray down on the altar in the middle of the Kirk, taking a moment to smooth out the edges of the embroidered towel. She sighs, almost inaudibly, looks to Luke, then to the painting of Jezebel, and then backs away.

Eve has a mean streak and feels no pity. It is the easier option, she knows, and she takes it anyway. It's not really her fault, for too long she has fed on a poisoned love – a sweetly nourishing toxin – and is unable to grow into a sense of herself that is bigger than the immediate. As she fits herself into the patterns of the Kirk, she struggles with their ideas of community and their demands to give and – worse – to accept. She sometimes thinks that she would just rather keep her share in a little bag and ration it out each day. But even there in the Kirk, where it is regulation to love, she finds that there are not so many ways to grow: the moulds available are Mother Loyola, the shrivelled bird-woman, or the younger versions with their tight mouths; docile, sweet Sarah who serves in love and speaks only to concur; and the bright, indulged, passionate Ana. Eve prefers at this point to make her own way.

The Brethren are talking easily as they enter the stone Temple – where are the serious, furrow-browed men that so unnerved Ana? Karl Kindali is wearing one of Eben's African robes, but he is much taller and it reaches only to his ankles. Eve, sitting in the pew, has a perfect view of his red socks as he sits on the golden chair near the altar. But as the chuckles fade, she sees that there is an anxiety, a restlessness that underlies the Brethren's humour. She turns her head to see a twelfth man standing at the back, almost beneath the image of Jezebel. He is wearing a hooded robe and looks up, as if pulled by her stare, with his weepy blue eyes – axe-murderer's eyes, the inconsolable eyes of a crying child. He sips his blessed wine.

"Who is that man who stands in the corner?" The words trip over her young clumsy tongue.

"He is the Traveller," Luke replies. "Nicolas Kumo. He is called the Wanderer, the Fallen One. He roams the world looking for signs and seeks the truth in unknown places. He is both the witness and the unseeing. His lot is to inhabit but be separate from the world that we have rejected. But he does so to search, to find the codes that he must unravel. It is his task, and his sons after him, to find the next message." Then, in a lower tone, Luke adds, "It has been a long while since we have had one."

Eve nods. She is intimidated and can't find her voice. "Why?" she wheezes. "Is something bad going to happen?"

Luke holds her hand with the barest pressure; Eve can't breathe.

The Traveller is welcomed by Karl Kindali and, beneath Jezebel, speaks out from the depths of the weepy blue.

"I have been to the ice mountains since we last met, and from there to the greenest forests. I have seen the vast beauty of the empty deserts, and the cruellest evils of modern man as hungry children lie waiting for death. I have gambled with the devil, been fed by the righteous and witnessed the suffering and joys of people in the deepest pockets of the world. All the while, I have kept my counsel and faith. I set off on my journey here to bring you my reflections on life that is unredeemed by the truth of the Kirk."

The Traveller takes out a leather-bound book and places it in the hands of Karl Kindali.

"This is what I have seen. Some of it will break your hearts, as it would have broken mine were it not already scattered in a thousand pieces. I journeyed here to tell you that no sign has been given. To make plans, for my time will run out in due course and I need to sow the seed for the next Traveller, who will search for the Word in my place when I am no longer able. But in the last stretch of my journey, something happened. It is for you to assess its meaning.

"I travelled down the length of Africa, relying on the kindness of strangers, by train, by minibus, by foot. It was a hot journey, even through the winter months. At times, I was a source of amusement in my robe; at other times, I caused a great deal of suspicion and on several occasions averted a near disaster through quick wit and fast legs, and of course through the benevolence of Malik, my guardian of light and protector."

The Traveller gestures and bows to the empty space beside him.

"I was making my way on foot through the Karoo when a white car pulled up alongside me. I was taken unawares. They seemed like good people, the man and woman who offered me a lift – which I did not accept as I was perceiving patterns in the veld and was content to walk along. They then said that they had trouble and asked if I could help them. I pointed out that I was just a poor traveller looking for answers. They laughed and said that was perfect: I would be the expert then. They too were travellers, they said, and had set out on a whim with no plan nor purpose. She wanted to go north and he south, and they had decided that they would go wherever the first person they saw would lead them. They stopped alongside the road with me a while, and offered me cordial and a sandwich.

"When I came to consciousness, I had been driven several miles and dumped, my body was stiff for being cramped into the back seat of the little car, and I had lost my robe, my wallet and most of the meagre possessions I had carried on my back. All that remained was my sacred book. I realise now that it was no accident; they were sent to me. If evil gives birth to good, if suffering brings us to the truth, I can only say God be praised."

The Brethren murmured their assent. The Traveller dropped his hood back and Eve was taken with his beauty, marred only by a wicked scar snaking down his temple.

"I was lying at the side of the road in a land I did not know. The landscape was impenetrable – it was the same brown earth and scrub whichever way I turned, and I despaired of ever finding my way out of this desolate region. I stood up to follow the path of the sun, which was scorching my skin. I collapsed again in a sorry heap and offered up the prayers for the dead.

"I thought Malik had taken human form and was quenching my thirst with an aloe leaf. I will never forget that moment of coming back to life in that barren brown land with the relentless sun, strong even at winter's four o' clock. I saw the vitality in all the other life forms around me as they were nourished by the heat and I imagined myself one of them, a slow lizard soaking up the sun, a dry bush drinking in the heat with such restraint. It was not Malik (though certainly sent by him) but a wizened little man of surprising strength, and between his granddaughter and himself, they managed to carry me about four miles to their cottage. I had lost a lot of blood and was a dead weight. I have only the barest memory of that journey to the house. Every time I returned to consciousness, I saw again and again the dry land, the patches of bush with endless koppies in the distance; we never seemed to reach them, they were always there, skipping back as we advanced. I spent a lifetime on that road.

"I recovered under the care of the old man and his granddaughter, Dulcie. They did not speak much English and so our communication was broken down to a most basic grammar of crude gestures. I spent three weeks there. The granddaughter had the lightest touch. Her skin was soft and her fingers firm but so very gentle. She cooked broths that my body craved, and later on a lamb stew fragranced with herbs that I didn't know existed. It was this delicious concoction that brought about my full recovery. But while I was staying there, a curious thing happened.

"Every night, just before her grandfather called her for bed, she would sit beside me with a bird – it was a strange bird, not very tame, one I have never encountered in all my travels, and I have seen a good many birds – and she would knit. The bird perched in an intricate wooden cage carved by the grandfather. She must have inherited his skill for detail, for her knitting was very meticulously crafted in a range of colours and each stitch was beautiful, carefully considered with attention to a some elaborate, half-revealed pattern. I asked her what she was knitting – it was getting quite long and was too wide for a scarf. Her response was morbid: a shroud. Each night as she knitted, the design took on a more distinct form. As the shroud neared completion, she became sadder and sadder until one night I found her in tears. When I pressed her about why she was crying, she told me that it was just too sad to say goodbye. And as I was getting better, I thought she meant me, for I detected a certain attachment on her part. But, lovely as she was, I had a duty to the Kirk and did not pursue this. On the night of the lamb stew, I was able to sit outside on the stoep, and here I found her casting off the stitches and finishing her shroud. She looked up at me and in a loud clear voice, in flawless English, she sang to me: 'The poison spreads from the inside. The agent of destruction is clothed in your colours. You will know this when the bees dance.'

"And as I watched, her bird became drained of colour and slowly shrivelled from the inside until all its feathers had turned to dust. Never have I seen anything like it: the poor creature was eaten up from the inside; all its organs destroyed themselves and it just imploded."

Karl Kindali is despondent, the Brethren look moodily around them. Eve thinks guiltily of her half-winged bird.

"We had been hoping for good news."

"We might have to cancel the Beesting. We can't have something go wrong."

"Something has already gone wrong," Eben sighs. Supper would be postponed, hopefully just half an hour.

"One of the initiates has accidentally killed a bee," Luke announces.

Oleander, small little flower, killer of bees and scapegoat, soon to be cast out and abandoned.

"She is just a girl," Luke says, "she means no harm."

"But we can't begin to guess the damage, this will ripple out and then where will we be? The whole Beesting is tainted by that dead bee. Eben, you're the scientist, you should know. We must cleanse the stain – you heard the Traveller. We will offer a sacrifice to the bees tonight to make reparation. That should do it. Just the Brethren, we don't want the whole Kirk muttering about this. And the girl must be gone before sunrise."

Oleander's burden is an unconscious toxin. Perhaps some snakes enjoy their bite, but maybe it is painful to kiss with a barbed tongue, to leak poison where one would spread love.

"I am declaring a Kirk retreat once the Beesting is over. Three weeks of fasting, and seal the community. No outsiders. Watch the other two. Get Luke and Thomas to keep a close eye on them."

"Mala's marriage to Tebogo will keep her under control, and we need not worry about Eve," said Eben.

Karl Kindali looked down at Eve – level with his red socks – for the first time.

"Nicolas, the time has come for you to take a wife," Eben said.

"We need to ensure that you have an heir to continue your work and your misadventure reminds us of the urgency of that. I would like to offer you the hand of one of our new initiates. Eve, we are offering you in marriage. With your consent, of course, which Luke has said you have given. You will travel with Nic until you have conceived, at which time you can return here to raise your children until they are ready. You will always have a home with us."

Eve thinks: but.

"I thought that I was to be a nun here, like Luke."

"Luke is not a nun, dear. What use is a nun? How can women serve men if they are nuns? Nuns are not much good to God. How can we then extend the Kumo, Kindali and Loyola lines if the women are becoming nuns? In any case, the Kirk does not have nuns. Perhaps you are thinking of a different god?"

Eve looks at Luke and thinks, hopes, she sees her desperation reflected in him. She cannot refuse. At least this way she will stay close to him, she will see him sometimes. Probably, she will have children and they will fear Luke Loyola as their preacher. At least there is that.

At seven o'clock, Oleander creeps out; she is heading for the bees. There is no one at the Beekeeper's lodge, they have all gone home. She has no idea of why she is going to the bees. There is spite on her mind, but also hurt.

It was an accident, she thinks, just an accident, and I was scared and is a person not allowed to make mistakes? She wipes away her snot (the wind is stinging) with her sleeve and trudges uphill to the hives. Once there, she doesn't know what to do — is she supposed to say sorry to the bees? But she is sorry, she is heartily sorry, she has never been more sorry in her life. She sits there for a while, and is lost in shadow as the sun descends behind the mountain. She can hear the low monotonous sound of the bees inside their beautifully ordered worlds, oblivious to their role in the Kirk's faith and in her demise. She forgets about this for a second as she thinks of them dancing inside the hive, and then thinks excitedly about seeing Eben entranced, dancing, covered from head to foot by the bees. Then she remembers: she will not be seeing the dance, and she aches with the pain of it. They will send her away in the morning and that will be the end of Oleander – who will she be then? It is too sudden – like a lover rejecting her, a world without warning coming to its end. She is not ready for this, only this morning she was encompassed tightly in the arms of the Kirk, and now, cold. It pains her too much to think of life in any other way; it is not possible. It is not the faith of the Kirk, that she has never really believed. She has loved Luke for years now, but even that has ceased to hurt – he will never take a bride. There is some solace in that. She thinks of his passion, of the beautifully delivered sermons in the stone Kirk, his lank hair swinging with his ardour. His delivery is quiet, even-voiced and solemn, almost as if he is reciting a shopping list, until he comes to the end, where he becomes more vehement, emphasising those last few lines as if the Kirk's salvation depended on it. And always he speaks of the same thing – love. But in different ways: she has heard his message of love through nature, through community and, most emphatically, through God. He is a good man, she knows that, and wonders what he would have been if not so bound by the regulations of his faith. If only the Kirk weren't so bloody uptight about this religion thing, she thinks crossly. And thinks some more. Then it occurs to her: she should respond to the religious with religion. Oleander ponders.

Eve walks with the Traveller later that evening. They wander up the hill and do not speak. They walk beyond the hives, they do not sense Oleander plotting in the darkened alcove behind the Beekeeper's Lodge. She sees it in his sidelong looks, his hand tentatively reaching to help her up a rock. In the Kirk there is no in-between. There is no courtship, no wooing, no lingering lovers' talks and excited heartbeats between unmarried and married. One day you are one and the next you may be the other. There is no divorce either, but there is wife disposal, a trickier tenet that may only be sanctioned by the leaders. How this happens is not entirely clear as it does not happen often. There are rumours of course, but these are invariably exaggerated and contain only a kernel of truth: wife disposal, not dissimilar to garbage disposal, involves depositing the burden in an appropriate unused space. And then there are the stories of millstones and cliffs. Eve does not like to think about that.

It should be a very good marriage; she should be happy. She has craved deserts and dry land, ice and snow; she has longed for variety of landscape, for space. There has been altogether too much green. As she looks around now and sees the sprinkling of ferns and long grass after the August rain, the fresh new spring growth before the summer sun bleaches to yellow, she thinks: I love but it stifles me.

And he is dry bones. He is without passion, without attachment. He can love and leave Dulcie (for Eve is sure that he does) and marry Eve all in the name of duty. Unbidden and without reason, Eve thinks: Nic's the devil's name, Nic's the devil's name and green is his colour. She suddenly panics: the Brethen were right, the traitor is from within. She would stop it if she could, if she had the strength, she would summon all the angels and devils she has known and she would call on them to get what she wants. For a moment, it seems almost possible that a wish would be enough. But then it is gone and she feels bereft. As she hears Nic talk of how happy they will be, of the world he would like to show her, she is suddenly impatient. She is impatient to say yes so that it can be over, and then he'll leave her be. She would have done her duty.

Then she sees Luke. Luke standing by himself in the shadow of a tree. Eve wonders if she is the agent of destruction. Have I come to destroy? Did I do it when I wasn't looking?

Luke is apologising for interrupting. He is unsure of himself, which is unusual for Luke who is always a steady presence in his black suit, like a crow, perched, coat-tails flapping. Eve is almost level with him but still, he will not look her in the eye, fidgeting instead with the black panama hat in his hands. It is almost tender, their silence, the things that are unsaid between them, as Nicolas talks of the big wide world and Eve sees Luke, loves Luke holding his black hat, under the tree.

It happens all at once: a terrible cry, a matted, stained creature with a torn yellow skirt hurling itself into Luke's arms (I have come to destroy) and the angry buzzing of bees. Eve and Nicolas run together to the hives beneath the ledge and there is a fire. Eve is not surprised: we have come full circle, it is that night all over again. Oleander is howling like a mad woman, screaming unintelligibly – words that don't make sense, that don't even sound like words. She thrashes about in Luke's arms and then breaks away and runs screaming. She is possessed. A crowd is gathering – word has spread through smoke signals, drumbeats on the ground. The mad buzzing of the bees – or is it the sound of the blood inside her head – is too close. There is Mother Loyola, a shroud over her head, screaming a silent scream. Ana runs with a bucket but the water splashes over her feet, over her skirt and the bucket is empty by the time she reaches the fire. Eben's brightly coloured robe is now dull and scorched.

Eve cannot see Luke; she panics, she must see Luke. The hives are drenched, leftover flames spit and black smoke rises. There he is: awkwardly holding up a limp Oleander who is too still, eyes staring unfocused ahead of her. The humming has stopped. Oleander's skin is red with blood and welts from the irresistible kiss of the bees. Her hands are burnt; they will be useless. Luke is straining as she convulses in a spasm, his face blackened with soot, his hat crushed in the soil and twigs. He is chanting a prayer. It starts softly beneath the clamour of the fire-fighters and grows in volume, as if by shouting he will make himself heard. Then suddenly he stops mid-word and looks confused. And sad, and Eve aches to make it better.

It is a flopped cake of a prophecy, banal in its treachery, pedestrian in its evil. But there it is, something has imploded. Tomorrow, there will be no Beesting.

B o n s a i

A ndrea regards the meaty rear of her cello and she is not pleased. It should be a dance, no? A light step, an arabesque maybe, a body curved backwards in a near-impossible arc. Possibly even walking on water, or clouds (the wisp is better); the lightness of a mathematical calculation. But it feels more like treading mud, or treacle – a sticky sweet thickness. The distance is unfathomable, she will not think through it. Instead, she turns her back, there is music to listen to: rock, pop or that horrible techno stuff – Mark has some somewhere, of course he does – or else, a housebound wife can never clean too much. A noisy washing machine, the vacuum cleaner, the chug of the refrigerator – which she suspects is on its last legs – scraping and scrubbing to drown out the silence, activity to detract from the stillness.

These are her companions on the journey. But she ends up on the couch again, the couch with a huge bag of Salt 'n Vinegar (25% extra), thinking ahead to the *koe'sisters* in the fridge, hidden behind the too-red steaks that Mark will insist on cooking for her tonight.

She doesn't bother with the second-hand thrillers hidden behind the cushions, nor with magazines. For now it is enough to look at the ceiling. There is much that can be told from ceilings – cryptic messages about the people living beneath them, sent up like smoke signals to those who come after. First there is the obvious stuff, like dirt or cracks. Her ceiling is spotless, even the light fitting is dusted once a month. Oh, she thinks, for a smidgen of dirt to read as if it were a tea leaf; a bit of rust or – she licks her lips – mould. What wouldn't she do for damp on her ceiling, raised bubbles of unsettled white like teenage skin. But it is like checking the letter box or the answering machine and finding it empty. At the far end of the room – she has to twist and her nightie bunches up beneath her –

there is a bit of paint peeling. Now that is exciting. She looks at the paint for a while but then the *koe'sisters* start getting impatient and she sets off to find them.

Andrea has a bonsai tree. It is a lovely little one, well cared for and clipped with precision. The only thing is that her bonsai lives inside her head. She visits it each day and snips and waters as she imagines one should with a bonsai. She places it within a bonsai garden, her little tree surrounded by friends. But best: she sings to her bonsai, she loves her tree with music. She has tenderly confined its roots and knows every detail of her little bonsai, beautifully stunted and gnarled with wise lines of growth. It is better that way, she thinks, to grow unobtrusively, to reject the bigger-is-better approach to things and to find an expression for these painful changes in another, more polite, way. That is why she is not too worried about success, or its lack, as she prefers quieter, more original means. But. It is not even success, after a while everyone stops wanting that. It would be enough just to do things, to get by, like go to a school and teach music to irritating little people who would rather not be torturing their instruments into pitiful squeals. For now she eats her *koe'sisters*, licking sticky coconut off greasy fingers, and thinks about cryptic things.

"Deceiver lures to secret place of thieves and beasts."

She can't figure it out. She asked Mark this morning but he was grazing on his bacon. Mark is big. Crossword, a funny name, she thinks, looking down at the empty grid. She tries the next and then the next but the moody black and white squares do not relent.

She is now sitting on the other chair, her legs draped over the armrest: it is time to examine the cracks in the skirting. It is noisy outside. Her concentration drifts easily and the sounds of the world getting on with things become unbearably loud. Children playing, the churning of a cement mixer, car alarms shrieking without abandon, the mournful cries of a mangy stray cat in the garden. She listens for a while and tries to hear the music there. But there is no music.

Instead, she is assailed by the noise outside, it feels like the sound of someone getting closer, crossing the elaborate barriers meant to keep unwelcome people out. That keep her inside – safe and sound. But the barbed wire and high walls sheltering the cottage are not necessary; Andrea keeps to herself regardless. They only disturb her sense of vision: she cannot see for the criss-cross lines, the untidy bundles of wire curled on the edges of the frame.

There are other things that threaten – the screams of the children down the street in the long, hot summer holiday. The indiscriminate shudders of the house. Sounds that could be the rattling of an upstairs window, the jiggling of locks, the muted footstep of a stranger on a loose board. But always, it turns out to be no one. Or the sounds of healing. Next door is a faith healer who heals very noisily. Bumps and grinds – accompanied sometimes by heavy drumming – move through the walls. She doesn't mind these noises too much; they can be quite comforting, once she knows it is not someone trying to get in. They are substantial sounds, unlike the shrill computerised beepy noises that make up the music of ordinary life. Ringing phones, alarms, tones, singing computer games, pinging microwaves, whistling muzak – everywhere there are thin tinny noises that irritate Andrea by their lack of resonance.

Not like her cello, that has resonance; so do the wheelie bins that are always being pushed around by the *bergies* who sit – gather? meet? – down at the corner of the street. To her it looks like they just laze about in the sun, making a noise, but who is she to judge that there is not some kind of complex social system operating. It probably has something to do with the wheelie bins. There are always wheelie bins stuffed with cardboard boxes being rolled about, an endless clanging on the gate (padlocked shut) for food. She doesn't even have a job to feed herself, how can she be expected to feed all the bloody homeless people as well? She never looks too closely if she ventures outdoors, but there is always an impression of wretched faces, usually a mosaic of cuts and colours – reds and magentas on lined skin. It would be nice to be able to help but where does one draw the line? She can't help them all. And what difference can one person make? But she knows that these are not her thoughts; they are easily available excuses, ready-made apologies, that she has heard and reused, sending them out like recyclable glass bottles or money. An anonymous system of exchange; a game of broken telephone played at dinner parties. There do not seem to be too many ways to stay separate – if she were to be truly honest – to draw the lines and seal herself shut from these people's lives. What is most uncomfortable is that the idea of such a life gradually takes on a terrifying ordinariness.

The *koe'sisters* were nice, she is full now. Mark always complains that she doesn't eat; she doesn't like to eat when other people, even her husband, are around. Her idea of a meal is a surreptitiously snatched bite of food that no one knows she is having. She has hidden junk food in different places all over the house, but she needn't bother – Mark doesn't really notice very much. She likes having secrets, it gives her a sense of purpose.

The sugar surges; Andrea wants to do something. She should be playing her cello, it would feel less sinful. It squats there in the corner – undisturbed for days – and Andrea doesn't notice herself going towards it. Then, a deep mournful groan, the grunt of a waking monster, pours through the walls and for a few startled seconds she almost thinks that it is the cello coming to life. To complain about its abandonment. Then it fades from a high intensity throb to a tired rattle, a sound she knows too well. She adds another complaint to her ever-growing list of things: the plumbing in this semi-detached piece-of-shit house Mark insisted on buying. Imperceptibly, her mouth curves just a tiny bit further down, her cheeks sag slightly and her chin drops the barest fraction. That faint line on her forehead tightens and settles itself more comfortably.

"Dear dear," she checks herself, "do I detect some hostility?"

But she has lost the way to the cello. It doesn't really matter. She is forlorn now: she doesn't really like herself.

"I am getting on my nerves," she laughs nervously. Then because the laugh sounds strange, she laughs again, only louder. That is how she catches herself: standing in the middle of the kitchen in her doughnut-stained nightie, belly bloated with junk, laughing like an idiot.

Usually, Andrea appears normal. She seems to be like most other people she knows: spoiled by a bit too much education; very nice acceptable liberal views (she would never admit that she calls the *bergies* "them", she is not even sure that *bergies* is an okay word anymore); a husband who doesn't indulge in passive-aggressive behaviour even if he chews loudly; a house that seems lovely if you don't actually have to live in it; two cars that work well, although she never uses hers because she never goes anywhere; they are thinking about children (crap, she hates the little fuckers). Andrea had a job – as a music teacher – but she lost it a few months ago and has been a bit bewildered since. Her yoga teacher – back in the days when she didn't mind leaving the house – told her that it was calming to nurture a garden in the head, that it was a good way to relax. But all Andrea could summon was a stunted tree whose roots she bound with a vicious strength. It took a while before she was bitter enough to create a whole garden. But now she loves visiting her little tree, it is her favourite thing.

She runs a bath – the pipes shriek happily – and she is calmer for running her fingers down the knobbly detail of her tree. She closes her eyes and sees the neighbouring trees, which are a bit less detailed than her special one, and raises her scissors to them.

A door slams so that the glass rattles. Andrea is up like a shot. She drips water as she fetches the towel she forgot to take into the bathroom. If someone has broken in, she thinks calmly, is it better to be dressed, or should I go and sort it out right now? Realising that she has no idea what "sorting it out" would entail, she opts for getting dressed. The fear sits in her throat and clogs her breathing. She is making her nervous way to the bedroom (she has a plan now: she can lock herself in and phone for help if anyone is downstairs) when she hears more slamming doors and screaming. The words are ugly and hurt and are launched with the precision of missiles. Andrea is relieved: it is not her fear; it is the healer next door.

A persistent tapping rises and recedes beneath the fury of next door's fighting; it is relentless. It is only when she is gathering the evidence of her indolence that she notices that someone is knocking at her door. She stands, chip packets and sticky coconut bag in hand, watching the glass shake with the tapping. She doesn't want anyone here.

Andrea opens the door a crack to find a dirty child standing there crossly. It is the girlboy child.

"How did you get in the garden?" She is annoyed.

The child is silent.

"What do you want?"

"Is the other one here?"

"What other one?"

"The other one."

"There is no other one here."

"Oh." The girlboy child stares at her.

"I'm very busy inside, so you'd better get going then. Okay?"

"Can I have an apple?"

"I don't have any apples."

"Can I have twenty cents?"

"I don't have twenty cents."

"Can I have – " It pauses, not sure what it is it wants; but it must continue the litany: "Some chocolate."

"Didn't your mother teach you to say please?" Andrea hears in herself the distant, unkind world of grown-ups.

"I don't have a mommy."

Oh, what is she to say to that? "Your daddy then?"

"He's in jail."

It is very thin, the girlboy child. And it holds its head high, nostrils slightly flared, twitching like a rabbit. No, Andrea checks herself: do not think in terms of animals. But it is skittish with large eyes, like a frightened Bambi. Disney characters, she reproaches herself, are even worse than animals.

"What is your name?"

"My name? ... Andrea ... what's yours?"

"Nicky."

Nicky the Orphan. A girl child. She holds her body in an awkward twist, tracing one dirty finger shyly around a diamond in the Trellidoor. Andrea sees the chipped nail polish on the chewed-down nails.

"I don't have anything for you today. Okay. Bye. And don't climb over the gate, that's very rude and little girls should have good manners."

What was she saying to the child! She thinks back to all the grumpy grown-ups that interrupted her child's world of play and taught her to sit still, wear nice dresses and feed little dollies. Anonymous adults in houses that bore imaginary "Keep Out" signs – don't play near them, they will chase you away.

"Can I come in?" A shy soft voice. She just wants to be friends.

"No." The certainty of the refusal embarrasses Andrea. "I have too much work."

And you are dirty. And my things are so pretty. And what is wrong with wanting to keep what's mine to myself? The lie makes her feel worse and she is sure that her cheeks are red from the telling of it.

"Pleeease."

It is a whine. Whining doesn't work with Andrea. It just makes her stick to her guns. Besides, she can see the specks of dirt that are being transferred onto the white diamond and she doesn't want Nicky inside and shedding germs from those suspiciously pink, colourant-stained fingers.

"Wait here."

She fetches some chocolate – it promises a quick return to peace and solitude – and unlocks the security gate. "If I give you this," – she is not without compassion – "you must go at once and never, ever come back. Okay?"

Nicky is squatting on the paving and when she sees the chocolate, she jumps up and stretches out, clapping both her hands.

"Who looks after you?" Andrea pulls the chocolate back.

"My ma, but she's old. And she's fat."

"Where do you live?"

Nicky points to a run-down block of flats rising in the distance. Andrea steps towards her and bends down. She feels vicious.

"If you ever, and I mean ever, come back here, I will go to your grandmother and tell her that you should be put in jail like your daddy and be whipped."

Her teeth are bared and she spits out the last word. Andrea bends closer; their faces are almost touching. She hopes that the nits don't jump across. She can smell the nasty smell of artificial flavours that children have, overpowering even the smell of stale cigarette smoke and old paraffin fires clinging to Nicky's clothes. Her hands hesitate above the thin shoulders. She regards the wide brown eyes and Nicky the Orphan suddenly seems a very tiny little girl beneath a too-high blue sky. Then Andrea sees the trickle and briefly wonders if Mark has turned on the fountain. The jagged wet line is running down the paving, from where Nicky stands, and forms a growing puddle at Andrea's lovely Italian sandals.

Andrea yelps. Nicky the Orphan rips the chocolate from the hands of the startled Andrea and leaps over the gate with alacrity. Andrea starts after her, but is not so indelicate as to climb over the gate. She turns back to the house to see the front door gently close and lock her out.

It is not easy getting over the gate in kitten heels. Also, it is slippery wet – something Andrea does not want to think about – and she feels a fool, perched on top of her gate. She hopes that the security patrol will not appear. After kicking off the heels – they land with a crack on the pavement – she makes it down the other side. But now she realises that she has no money, no place to go. She pauses on the pavement, wondering which way is best. It is hot outside and there are people sitting at the corner of the street, but they pay no attention to her. It is simple, she tells herself. Just go to one of the neighbours and call Mark and tell him to come home to let you in. But all the chip packets and sweet wrappings will be in full view.

Bells jingle as she walks through the half-open door of the neighbour's house. It is quiet and when Andrea calls out, her voice resonates down the empty passage. No one answers and she continues down the passage, peering into the empty rooms on the left. At the end of the corridor, she pushes through a door and hears a dejected voice from the corner of the room.

"This room is auspiciously positioned for healing."

Andrea sees the man sitting in the corner; he does not look well. She doesn't think that she would trust him to heal her. He wears a white robe, but it looks more the prayer robe her Muslim great-uncle wore than a doctor's coat. And even though men in dresses don't usually do it for her, she notices that he is a very attractive doctor.

"That comfortable?" She points to the robe.

He does not reply but starts walking towards her, slowly and as if deep in thought.

"You are not well," he says, reaching for her hair. He takes a strand and sniffs it.

"Actually, just locked out."

"I am the key. I can open all your doors. I will find what has been hidden behind all the junk of life, and bring you release."

Perhaps, Andrea thinks as she finds herself gently lowered onto his healing bed, that might be quite nice.

"There are seventy-six known ailments that I can treat through realignment."

Doctor Gordon's hands are hovering above her head, not touching, and she feels a strange burning at the crown, spreading through her hair.

"There is only one, the seventy-seventh, that has flummoxed me. I have searched high and low to find a cure for miscommunication but just can't seem to get it right."

His hands are burning a slow beam into her shoulders now, and she feels something stirring. It comes to her now: liar. Or is it lair? Lured into the den of iniquity.

"I have been to many places, learned from many great men. I spent a long time with John Two Trees Romero and his child brides. He would only speak a sentence every few days and even this was whispered to me, amidst much giggles from the child brides. He knew the art of communication."

Slowly he moves his hands down – not touching her skin – and she glows wherever he doesn't quite touch her. Sleepily, she says to him: "I have a bonsai."

In her mind she sees her bonsai. There it is in her little garden – as it always is – and she is singing to it, loving it. She feels a surge of love and reaches for the tree, impatient to touch it. She runs her hands through the details of her bonsai, first the knobbly bark, then those leaves that are just the right shade of green. Then she sees the brown flecks on the bark of one of the branches. Frowning, she sees that they are wood lice – or what she imagines are wood lice – and pulls them off. But then she sees that the next branch is also covered, and the next – the whole tree is being nibbled upon. Even as she pulls them off, ripping bark and leaves at the same time, more appear. Frantically she looks around at the other trees. They too are covered in lice. She sees a furious scrabbling around the roots of her tree – it is loose in the soil. She shakes the insects from her hands, which are covered in dark specks. Andrea lifts her beloved bonsai from the infested garden and starts walking. In her mind she is walking and walking but doesn't know where she is going. It feels nice to be leaving and she doesn't mind that Mark is not with her. The sense of boundless space as she walks unfamiliar paths fills her with a deep excitement. Just her, Andrea alone, balancing a bonsai in the palm of her hand as she sets off over hills of glass and through magical forests.

Andrea opens her eyes and sees the doctor's hands fluttering down. She smiles at him. She closes her eyes again and, to a deep distant harmony, Andrea dances on with her bonsai.

E n d p i e c e

They wanted to tell their story but did not know where to start. It seemed there could be no beginning that was not founded on some other beginning. But this way, all possible sources seemed too remote. This story could not be told without footnotes, endnotes, little asterisks inserted between every word to refer to another, to carry their story the way the stars carry the sky. Their story wanted a map to trace each stop visited and revisited, to wind through every destination only to reveal it as the point of origin. Each stop punctuated their tale with the arbitrary deliberation of a rusty nail puncturing a tyre. Any of these stops could be the start. They had to decide on a beginning. They decided to start here.

They drove along the grey road towards the setting sun. Luke's arm rested lazily on the steering wheel, his fine brown hairs lit by the late afternoon. They had passed fields with young crops, others with animals grazing, driven by great stony hills and along deep green mountain byways. For all that, Eve could not discern much difference between here and there. All brown knolls seemed vaguely the same to her; in every field there were new plants tied to their wooden crosses. Yet each time she saw these features repeat themselves, she delighted in their beauty. The snaking road seemed to eat its tail as she saw yet another distant cottage, and wondered again who lived there and what they did all day. She traced the gnarled granite faces of the mountains flanking them on either side; she regarded the textures of clouds gliding far above. As they drove, she left her thoughts on the pictures before her, only to have them fly back and weave themselves into her – when it seemed that the car had simply returned instead of going forward. She had hoped that she could leave her thoughts behind – that as they drove, she could simply empty her mind as though emptying a litter bag, that the thoughts would be whipped away by the wind; but they got lodged in the trees, where they hovered, waiting for her return.

She would have liked to not return, to find new places. But by trying to get lost, they somehow kept finding the road home. Eve looked at Luke's arm almost imperceptibly steering the car, at ease on the wheel after so many months of driving in circles, and felt that perhaps their story began when at last they accepted the necessity of their return.

Or it could have started with that painting. Luke could not say for certain if it was then that the questions began, but that was when he first noticed them. It hovered above the mantelpiece – a bold cry in apocalyptic white – and crowded the simple room. A wooden desk stood in the corner, bearing a vase of garden-picked flowers. The weekly scripture lessons (and more) were there in that one picture. It spoke more immediately to the Kirk schoolboys than Luke's thin unimpassioned ramblings about seven and a half rings of hell and mortification of the flesh. That too-bright picture brought home the temptations of the flesh – how her robe fell against the curve of her body. And about punishment, it was more than explicit. The groaning imps in the bottom left corner reaching towards that gown with avarice and glee; the dark abyss beneath the edge of the cliff with the mucky green waves waiting to swallow her. Above, the sad angels alongside an older version of Luke in the dark suit and top hat piously praying, hands raised. The boys understood enough. Heaven and all its angels were there, but in not quite as much detail as Hell. But even angels and devils, spirits and the saintly Kirkers perched on the upper right were diminished by the Whore of Babylon, Jezebel herself, hair whipping about her face. Her diaphanous robes, lifted by the wind, swirled around her. She stood at the top of the grey cliff, overlooking the sea, overlooking the room. But instead of appearing wicked and remorseful, she seemed rather nice. She seemed a normal, friendly kind of girl, one that you wouldn't mind living next door, Luke thought. Jezebel appeared to have not quite registered her fate and looked out with a sensible if slightly uncertain stare.

Luke had found it increasingly difficult to work at the desk when preparing his sermons. He used to like working there, he found a deep delight in the warmth of the morning sun and the blue of the sea. They had called him from that room, from his meditation, the artist and Jezebel, the day they delivered the painting. Mr Farmer had wrapped it in layers of bubble-wrap and brown paper. The woman who was with him, the woman in the painting, had stood by – quiet and ordinary – in the dark reception passage. At first, she was hardly noticeable next to the big man who filled the room. He perceived that she wore trousers, an unpleasant trait in women and one which the Kirk did not encourage. But then she looked up at Luke and smiled at him. Very sweetly, he smiled back at her, almost bemused. They left and he put the painting aside to work until Ana came in and cooed with delight. The wrapping paper was torn into shreds as if Ana were enraged, as if it were a present, and she gasped and sighed her pleasure. Ana was as pretty as a dolly: if he lay her down, would her eyes shut and would she go to sleep?

He wished he had not seen her, the woman in trousers, for now he could not look at the picture without thinking of her. It was unnerving to have a demon wear the face of an ordinary woman. This is what he first thought. Every now and then, he was struck with the knowledge that somewhere this Jezebel was eating, sleeping and doing undemonic things. He began to wonder if the painting had affected her in any way. She was forever entrapped in this image of Jezebel before her demise, she did not deserve that.

The painting became a shrine to Ana and her girlfriends who would visit religiously, their glossy mouths gaping. Eben encouraged her, saying, "That's why we commissioned the painting, we want these impressionable young minds to learn." Luke glanced up from his desk in the corner as they paraded through the room. He looked at them sternly from beneath his glasses so that the tentative giggles would taper off. He had a vague suspicion that it was not so much the religious lesson that appealed to Ana and her friends, though they would never admit it. Indeed, they probably did not even know it. He suspected that it was not entirely disapproval that informed their desire to visit, but desire itself that drew them there. He could not voice these blasphemous fears to Eben. But when those girls stood before the painting and shook their heads in disparagement, he sensed something stronger, something forbidden, something resembling awe in their muted appraisal.

Luke disapproved of the visits and he disapproved of the painting. He tried not to look at it but found himself, like the young girls, drawn to the picture. When he wrote his sermons at the desk, she would be waiting for him to look up while pausing to think. He could now read exasperation in her eyes: why do I have to endure this idiocy? she wanted to say. But she couldn't because she was frozen in one unfortunate moment, a moment that perpetually held her as an object of derision and scorn. And unarticulated desire. He felt sorry for her, he wanted to undo the ropes that bound her hands. He wanted to tell her that his Kirk – Luke's Kirk – would never really hurt anyone, they just threatened to hurt them. But a feather-thin tear appeared in his reasoning: what was the difference, even if Jezebel were not thrown off the cliff? Even if they unbound her hands and sent her home, it was too late. Luke could determine no terror in her face. And again: how could she? How could that woman, who smiled so sweetly and wore trousers without a second thought, how could she continue a nice ordinary unfettered life if there was forever an image of her as enslaved by evil, about to be punished by good? It was that moment of suspension that most offended Luke; if only it was just after the punishment, at least then she would be released. But instead she had to always anticipate the dreaded moment. He willed the figure to run away. "Go on then, defy them," he said aloud, perched on the edge of his desk, top hat in hands, coat tails neatly hanging down the side. "Don't let those fools bully you, you look infinitely more sensible than they do."

She stood there for many months, mildly bemused. Even if she could run, she would probably trip over those ridiculous robes and hurt herself. Luke took to sitting on the green velvet chair beneath the painting while writing, so that he did not have to look up at her. But he could still feel her above him, as if she were gently alive and softly breathing.

When he began preparing for the Beesting, Luke's writing increasingly became a fragmented reflection on freedom and discipline; there were urgent words on punishment and love. Eben was displeased when he read the Beesting sermon – it questioned too much; it was not from God. Eben rewrote the sermon and took the picture off the wall. He was beginning to wonder about graven images and feared that there may be a danger in the image of a demon woman. He put it in a closet, face to the wall.

"But I need to be reminded of evil and its punishment," complained Ana sweetly.

"Probably just makes her feel worse to be shut up in the closet anyway," Luke moped.

Eben told Luke to pull himself together and not behave like some wet-behind-the-ears schoolboy. He decided that the best place to hang the picture was in the Kirk itself, in consecrated space, just in case. And on the day that the Beesting should have been, on that darkest day, as Luke stood up to recite the rewritten sermon, he looked up to see Jezebel, who hung demurely at the back of the Kirk. He faltered as he spoke and then without realising that he remembered, the forbidden sermon came to his mouth and delivered itself.

A quiet voice, an amused voice spoke out.

"But that wasn't exactly how it happened. You're remembering just what you want to remember – the fall of the great messenger of God, how Luke Loyola lost his religion."

This was perhaps unkind of Eve. There was no one moment when Luke decided that his God was not there and switched off his love for his Kirk. Even now, his doubts were not confirmed, his uncertainty not made certain. There remained a struggle beneath his apparent choices, as he craved too many things he had left behind. He was only steady in an awareness of what could not be: he could not continue in the Kirk, he could not not love. His link with God had slowly faded, like ink steadily exposed to light: a comic book on a summer windowsill; a telephone connection made inaudible by static. But it was not entirely erased or blotted out: just distant, unreachable across debris and fragments of hesitation – the shattered remains of rigid structures and denial. If Luke chose to connect his loss of faith to the picture, it was because it could hold and contain the incident of forgoing all that was love to him. It made some sense of the puzzle. It allowed him to tell the story that he did not quite know, but for the final line which said: I have lost, I am without. Another love expanded then – Luke was a good man and had enough love for both God and Eve.

"It started with a picture but not that one, it just continued with that one. Besides, the Whore of Babylon was hardly as commanding as you make it out to be. It was quite poor, really."

"But it attracted gaggles of girls to ogle at it."

"Oh no, my sweet, it was you who drew the girls."

There was another picture, a humbler attempt to capture some rocks hiding behind the sea, which marked a different beginning. Every morning on the beach, Eve struggled to translate the rockiness of the huge boulders into her drawings. She sketched them in pencil and charcoal, tried watercolours and pastels, but she could not coax the substance from the rock onto her paper. She was determined to capture these rocks that moved her so, so she did not do the sensible thing and move on to something else. But they remained elusive; she only ever managed big sandy brown lumps. It was possibly the elusiveness that compelled her to continue. Perhaps it was not so much the rocks that drew her, but a desire for precision; she wanted to apprehend the elusions. Whatever her reason, Eve worked doggedly on the beach.

There were people who walked that beach regularly, like the old woman with the golden retrievers and the skin shrivelled from her morning swims. There were people who walked the beach occasionally, like the old man with heavily veined legs and a walking stick. There were people whom Eve had never seen before, and then some who seemed familiar, although she could not say why. The girl with the pretty brown curls and the hand-knitted cardigan was one of these. She approached Eve timidly, asking if she was an artist.

"Not really," Eve replied, "I just try."

The girl, her name was Ana, confessed that her greatest desire in life was to be an artist, but she would never be allowed to attend the art school because her father said that they were filled with subversive types, and gays and lesbians. And she was called to a different path – it was a very important path because she had important blood. Eve felt a certain mutuality between them, even though her blood was not important, in fact, so unimportant that it lay scattered without a trace. They spoke all morning and then Eve had to return home because it was lunch-time. The next day, Ana came to the beach again, wearing another hand-knitted cardigan.

It was after Ana started painting the rocks that Eve realised they would never get them right. This was because the rocks themselves were wrong and resistant to being captured. This was apparent from Ana's flat attempts. So instead they found different stretches of beach, went for hikes up the hill, looking for the right rocks. There was some recognition of the possibility that perhaps it wasn't the fault of the rocks, that maybe they weren't very good at drawing, but it gave them an excuse to meet whenever they could with a light-hearted mission.

It was Ana's most enduring proof that in her brother's workroom, there was a painting of extraordinary merit. Somehow the possession of this work lent credibility to her less extravagant attempts. She spoke of it with great reverence and eventually clutched Eve's arm and said in a low voice, "You must come and see it, you must." It was not simply the fine artistry that appealed to her; she felt it spoke to something inside her that she could not pinpoint.

Eve was sneaked into the Kirk Hall along with some other girls in home-made dresses. She stood amidst them in the upstairs room and felt their awe as they regarded the picture. The image of Jezebel evoked a vague recognition, but it was discordant and remained out of reach. But Jezebel in all her finery did not command Eve's attention as much as the quiet man on the other side of the room. Luke Loyola sat in the corner of the room at a wooden desk. He looked at them sternly over his glasses – that made Eve want to giggle. It was not the garish religious decorations that caught her eye, it was the preacher himself that she found inspiring.

Perhaps it began with the downward curve of a lip, the light crease next to a black dancing eye. The remnants of an older, tireder face peering out of this smaller, less worn one. For they may not have shared blood but something lingered, perhaps a mannerism: the shrug of her shoulders, the toss of her hair that Eve had unknowingly stored away. Or it could have been transmitted through love and longing. There was a likeness: one was an extra child, the spare daughter, nurtured by the stepmother's venomous love, that swelled the family and then turned malignant. The other was the only child, the stolen child Evie, who was elusive and longed for. There was a likeness but no one to appreciate the similarities. Did they pass each other on the street, at a restaurant, the theatre? Jessica was sure that she would know – she always hoped to find Evie, but never looked for her. She did not know what she would do if she encountered her. She suspected that the much-anticipated reunion would most likely not be the running, hugs and kisses she had once imagined. What would they talk about? That moment after too many lazy years when a burdened Jessica looked at herself and screamed very quietly: what have I done? What does an aunt who once fiercely loved her sister's child say after so many strange years? Jessica knew only small talk.

In fact, they did pass each other one summer night at the theatre. If she had been a few seconds later, Jessica would have seen Eve walk up to Stephen at the theatre door. Eight years later, it would have taken effort to recognise Eve: to trace the changes from the gawkiness of puberty to the finely chiselled woman who now walked towards Stephen. But Stephen she would have remembered. If Jessica had seen Stephen she would have stared at his thinned-out hair, his wiry body that was now too lean and shrunken. She would have paused a moment, then sighed as she again realised her bad taste in men; then remembered that he was even more vile than she. And those anxious, angry words that had so long waited to be said might have risen and then subsided as she thought, why bother, I don't want to cause a scene.

But Jessica was too early; when Stephen was walking towards Eve from inside the theatre door and Eve was approaching him from across the foyer, Jessica had just walked by. She did not see the young woman advancing, nor the man stepping forward, intending to kiss the woman's cheek and hand over the tickets.

It was Stephen who noticed Jessica drifting through the foyer. He watched her walk past, and became agitated. Eve was surprised to find her father so worked up. He refused to take his seat: he needed his glasses, he was thirsty, he had a migraine. Stephen insisted they go home right away but Eve pointed out, quite reasonably, that they could not leave if he was so ill. She did not know how to drive and it was far better if he calmed himself first. Eve was always calm. The theatre doors were closing and a few people slipped inside just as they shut. Eve and Stephen stood in the empty foyer. She then steered him to the tea-room and sat him down. She ordered for them and went to the toilets, where she saw Jessica.

Eve saw Ana's painting come to life when she saw Jezebel in a short white dress applying lipstick. She couldn't place it at first: there was a recognition, and Eve wondered if she was one of the people she had known before, that haunted the corners of her mind. But then she remembered – the room at the Kumo Kirk, with the big painting above the green chair, where the serious preacher wrote about God.

147

Eve was always too shy to look in public mirrors – it made her feel vain. She took off her Alice-band and then put it on again, pushing her long hair back. There. Then as she waited in the queue, she watched the sad-faced Jezebel in the mirror. Jezebel seemed removed, unaware of the room around her, intent only on applying her lipstick. Eve wanted to go to her, started towards her, but then for no good reason turned away. She just decided that she would rather not. Then she decided that she did not want to pee and left the toilets. As she reached Stephen, she decided that she did not want the sweet tea either.

She went to Stephen as he sipped his tea and said very kindly, "I have to go now. I am sure that you can understand."

She turned from him and walked away; the image of him wiping his mouth with the white cloth was the last she saw of him. Stephen followed her as she walked through the big revolving door into the evening air. But it was no ordinary night: it looked like Armageddon with the sky scorched by fire – ash and soot swirling in the wind and settling on her hair. Stephen called after her but she did not turn around. She walked all the way to the train station before his cries were snatched away by the wind and scattered so that she could no longer hear them. She caught the evening train to Simon's Town and walked through fire to the Kirk Hall to find Ana. False Bay was in flames that night – a chaos of cars and people watching as the mountain burned. The train slowly chugged towards the heart of the heat and Eve was not afraid.

Perhaps it began with a raised eyebrow, with words spoken out of lips pushed to the side of the mouth. There were two pairs of deep black eyes that became one for Luke. She had the fragility of someone who had just walked out of a cage – or stepped from a picture. There was something uncertain yet bold in her movements – as if she expected to fight invisible walls blocking her way. Luke felt he needed to show Eve as much space as he could. First he took her to open fields, then large stretches of beach and then wide open farmland. When that was not big enough, they travelled to the Karoo – there they found that they had so much space to discover together that they kept moving through most of the country and further still. It was never enough.

But meeting each other was not what they considered to be their story – that fell between words. And if it was a love story, that was incidental. In any case, Luke believed that all stories were love stories one way or another. Eve put this down to his religious upbringing. But the past was done, and could not be revisited in ways any more substantial than flickers of light imprinted inside their eyelids. It was too inconstant, as it was reduced over time, changing from one imagining to the next, until just the bare bones of their telling remained – a pencil sketch. It changed also from Luke to Eve, from Eve to Luke; what had happened was reduced to impressions and then, as they told it to each other again and again, to the sum of their impressions. They had created a new story, which was no less real. But the future – that was different. They wanted a happy ending, they insisted upon it.

They were almost home now. The road had been curbed into one dull line, dutifully bearing its travellers home without any sly twists. Eve was beginning to recognise familiar features: the wood and zinc houses, the dry, shadeless land, then the huge salt-and-pepperpot towers, the black Black River, then the mountain coming closer and closer. This mountain she knew. Entering the shadow of the mountain, she felt some relief at their return. When they reached the mountain, they turned with it and drove along the gently winding road, tucked in its folds. They did not spare a thought for those they had left behind, for those who were left without.

NOTE:

The Kumo Kirk is a gnostic sect whose unique beliefs and rituals can be traced back to Christian and Manichean origins. Their doctrine of faith emphasises spirit over matter. The Kirk was founded in 1780 by Elijah Kumo who experienced a series of dreams, visitations and hallucinations that has been associated with an attempt to make a mushroom jam (see Hoffmeyer in *Spirit Matters*, Summer 1975). Elijah Kumo started the Kirk with his wives Hannah and Karen, their father, Christopher Kindali, and his three sons. They travelled around Europe until settling in a small town, possibly near the Harz Mountains, where they established a community. Elijah Kumo's grandson, Elias, believed himself called by God to Cape Town in the early 1800s, where he married his housekeeper, Yasmien (who converted to Kirkism from Islam) and had nine daughters. The strong Islamic influence on the Cape Kirk is evident in many of the rituals that developed there. The eldest daughter, Serai, married Rafiek Suleiman, who became Lucas Loyola when he converted. They had eight children, after which Lucas Loyola ritually disposed of his wife to become the first monk of the Cape Kirk. Heske Loyola married Nicolas Kindali, the Traveller, and had seven children. Three of the sisters married Tebogo Cann the Elder, who fathered seventeen children. The second son, Lucian, who took the Loyola name, was a monk, preacher and leader of the Kirk. He established the Beekeeper's Lodge beyond Red Hill. Antje Cann married Altan Loyola; their only child, Lucius Loyola, a monk, abstained from his abstinence in order to ceremoniously father Eben Loyola – he dutifully impregnated seven women during a weeklong procreation fest; Eben Loyola was the only pregnancy carried to full term. He is the current leader of the Cape Kirk and is married to Sarah Loyola (née Kindali) and they have three children: Luke, Ana-Clarissa and Rebecca. Private communities now flourish in nine countries across the globe. The Kirk communities are exclusive and invitations to the sect are now rare.

ACKNOWLEDGEMENTS:

An earlier variation, *Fugues*, was written with the help of the Centre for Creative Writing at the University of Cape Town, where I received tremendous support. I single out John Higgins, at least for the finer points of punctuation; and Daniel Roux, an ideal reader.

On the margins of these stories (quilts), between the lines, lay the support, advice and care of so many; several conversations have helped me piece together the background. I thank Annari, Anne-Marie and Henrietta at Kwela and Ashraf at the Writer's Network for excellent midwifery. In Bristol, Peter Metelerkamp and Naomi Smyth amongst others helped me to prune "Bonsai" through filming *Andrea's Variation*.

For kind words of encouragement and support beyond all expectations, since its earliest inception, my deepest thanks to André Brink. And for sharing story worlds with me, I am grateful to Cathal Seoighe – we talk them alive.